Last Trolley from Beethovenstraat

Other Verba Mundi titles

The Lonely Years, 1925-1939
by Isaac Babel

The Tartar Steppe
by Dino Buzzati

The Obscene Bird of Night
by José Donoso

The Book of Nights
by Sylvie Germain

The Prospector
by J. M. G. Le Clézio

Honeymoon
by Patrick Modiano

The Christmas Oratorio
by Göran Tunström

Last Trolley from Beethovenstraat

GRETE WEIL

Translated from the German by John Barrett

Verba Mundi
DAVID R. GODINE, PUBLISHER
Boston

First published in the U.S. in 1997 by
David R. Godine, Publisher
Box 9103
Lincoln, Massachusetts 01773

Published in German as *Tramhalte Beethovenstraat* by
Verlag Nagel & Kimche AG, Frauenfeld, Switzerland, in 1992.
First published by Limes Verlag, Wiesbaden, in 1963.

Library of Congress Cataloging-in-Publication Data
Weil, Grete, 1906–
[Tramhalte Beethovenstraat. English]
Last trolley from Beethovenstraat / Grete Weil ; translated
from the German by John Barrett.—1st American ed.
p. cm—(Verba Mundi)
ISBN 1-56792-032-4 HC
I. Title. II. Series.
PT2647.E4157T713 1995
883 .914—dc20
95-35209
CIP

First American edition
This book was printed on acid-free paper
Manufactured in the United States of America

Last Trolley from Beethovenstraat

Chapter 1

SUSANNE entered without knocking, thrusting her belly slightly forward, an archaic smile on her lips. But she wasn't smiling. With large, round, amber-yellow eyes she motioned toward the desk and said, answering her own question, "No."

He hastily shut the notebook lying in front of him. A schoolboy, caught. She went to the bookcase, took down the three volumes of his work, which she considered her most sacred possessions, pressed them tenderly to her breast, and said, once more, "No!"

For years she'd been saying the same thing. As usual, his reaction was to hate her: unjustified hate, because she couldn't help it if she no longer looked like an Arab boy, ragged, half-starved, with the ravenous look of someone who'd been kicked around in one of the camps. She had filled out to the point where she had what men at the beach called "a great figure." No one could swim all the way across the lake or the entire bay as she did, with powerful strokes, almost without exerting herself. Beaming, she would climb onto the shore and pull the swimming cap from her black hair. Victory all down the line. Defeat only where he was involved. She had married a poet. *"Mon poète."* The author of two volumes of poetry and a novella. In the new *Brockhaus Encyclopedia*, he was listed as a "young, very promising prewar lyric poet."

Susanne could afford to give him the material security that in her view an artist needed. The estate of her gassed parents was huge and she was the sole heir. She'd made the sacrifice of moving to Munich for him, to that hateful country, because she thought a German poet ought to live in German surroundings. Built a house in Grünwald and put him in a room with soundproof walls.

But he wasn't writing. That was beyond her understanding. She considered it a deliberate insult.

He pushed his chair back and stood up. Walked over to the painting by Klee—yellow birds and an orange crescent moon—that actually came from her family, but belonged to him. His only possession. It was unframed, tattered along the edges, and a tear ran from one corner to the other. "You just don't hang up torn pictures," she'd said at a time when they were still speaking to one another, as he was putting it up on the wall with thumbtacks.

He screwed up his courage in front of the partially decapitated and tailless birds, before turning around.

"Can I have the car for a few days?"

"No."

"Give me the keys."

"No."

Then he became aggressive, something very unlike him. She always carried the keys to her car—which next to his books she loved most—with her. The surprise attack succeeded, the books kept her from defending herself. He pulled the keys from her skirt pocket.

"No!" The angry screeching of a peacock. And then, sobbing wildly: "No!"

The door slammed shut. He ran to his bedroom, grabbed the already packed bag, and carried it to the garage.

The gardener opened the gate for him as he backed out the red Porsche.

"Is the Gentleman leaving without Madam?" He didn't answer, put off by being addressed this way, in the third person.

He bumped against the gatepost with the right rear fender. Instead of manuevering away carefully, he gave it the gas. The post scraped along the whole side of the car. So what? Nothing interested him but the street that led away from Susanne's house, a street of rich businessmen and movie actors. He was not so presumptuous as to think,

"To freedom." He simply thought, "Away." Nothing else. Long since accustomed to the fact that his actions were of no consequence.

The best thing about an automobile was that it drowned out the rolling noise of the trolleys. But at a traffic light that was changing from red to green, he heard it anyway; terror crept up his spine, he forgot to pull away, horns started blowing behind him, the car lurched forward, a man jumped aside and tapped his finger against his forehead.

It was good to drive. Concentration keeps you from being over-sensitive. You think as others do, simplistically, egotistically, inconsiderately. Porsche drivers greeted each other by flashing their headlights, a band of speedy conspirators. The first time, he forgot to return the greeting; the second time he responded; by the third time, he was the first one who blinked.

He drove by the museum. His father, in a professorial slouch hat, had guided the nine year-old and lectured with a raised voice—as if he were speaking to his students in an auditorium—about the gothic madonnas, all slightly bowed down, overly slender; each one looked just like all the others, wooden, in front of whitewashed walls, smiling insipidly in eternal motherhood. Horrible boredom. He nodded drowsily at his father's words and let the marbles click against one another in his pants pocket. Then they came to a corner, around which death was waiting on horseback, shimmering blackly, with bared teeth, scythe and hourglass in hand. It was the first time he'd seen it. The confrontation was a stormy one, left a burn on his flesh that never healed, and, at a single stroke, put an end to the time of comforting security.

"A mediocre work. Come along, Andreas." But he didn't come, couldn't come, his legs were too weak. He reached out his hand, grabbed at Death's gaunt nag, all cold and hard. Something untouchable, something forbidden. He drew his hand back, crept after his father, who was waiting impatiently: "There's no use taking you along, you're still too stupid."

But after a few days, censure was transformed into praise. He went to the museum, uninvited, alone, just as often as he could. His mother told the other women over tea, and they shook their heads with admiration and concern at such precocity. "But not to the nativity scenes, as you might think, no, to the gothic madonnas. Right, my little man, you're happy in the presence of those beautiful women?" He nodded, prepared to lie in order to protect his secret. *"Épatant, il a seulement neuf ans,"* said the wife of the Trade Commissioner, who apparently thought it impossible that a child could understand French.

The madonnas lined the way like dark cypresses leading to a cemetery; high above him, they smiled as he ran by without looking at them, with a pounding heart that beat faster and faster as he came closer to the corner. There he stopped, all doubled up, paralyzed, trembling with horror and desire, and savored the torment of waiting. Sometimes he could only stand it for a moment, but at other times he even managed to prolong the torture. Not yet, not yet, not yet, soon now, just about now, one, two, three, four, five, six, seven— now! Then he would break into a run, throw a harried glance at the dark figure, and flee.

Always the same ritual, for months, for years, until he began to write his first poems. Hymns to death, in free verse; Novalis and Mombert were his models.

He stopped in front of the house that had belonged to his parents, in the Herzogpark, around the corner from Thomas Mann's. Burned out, it had been sold by his father for next to nothing before the currency reform. The new owner had modernized it without making it any more attractive; you could still see its art nouveau origins despite every attempt to cover them up.

He stayed in the car for a while, then climbed out, walked over to the fence, and looked into the garden, which was no longer the beautiful wilderness of former days, but an affected imitation of a park in much too small a space. A Japanese cherry tree in full bloom, lilac bushes—but they had been there even in his day—a few exotic pines with soft, hanging needles, rhododendrons and azaleas; on the closely mowed lawn two children were playing with colored hoops.

The little girl, about eight years old, and the somewhat older boy threw mistrustful glances at him. For a moment it looked as if the boy would come over to the fence and tell Andreas to leave; but then he made an imperious movement with his hand and forced the girl to go on playing. At that age, Andreas would have rejoiced over every stranger. Everyone who came brought great adventure, everyone was a messenger from the gods, someone you received with enormous readiness to be enchanted.

This boy had decided that a man who looks through the bars into other people's gardens was not worthy of attention. He went on playing with complete concentration, tyrannizing the girl and making use of the slightest advantage. How good it would have been if he'd cheated! But he didn't cheat, didn't need to; calculatedly he got what he wanted. This openly displayed superiority was unfair and brutal. He was using his little sister in order to develop his skill for coming out on top. She was a kind of punching bag that he beat against to strengthen his muscles. A useful object, not something to love.

A foreign generation. Just as foreign as his parents. In between, lost, he himself.

His father's pathetically sobbing voice when he spoke about mankind. Professor of Medieval History at the university. A Wagner expert, Wagner afficionado, hojotoho, Schiller might measure up to his standards, too. Latin gushed out just like German, Greek was reserved for recitation. A little French, no English. Without interest in other countries unless it was something to do with the medieval period. A philistine who characterized himself as an upright democrat and everyone else as philistines; vindictive, a believer in progress, con-

7

vinced that the Germans and above all, the Bavarians, were the zenith of creation. For his mother, the daughter of a rich Silesian mill owner, democracy was a matter of indifference; she was inclined toward the nobility. Two Wittelsbach princes belonged to the circle of their closest friends. Even a few Jews—one must be tolerant. Hitler they couldn't stand, made fun of him, openly at first, then, later, secretly, *"Attention les domestiques."* On official occasions they raised their arms in the German salute, even made their contribution to the Nazi "Winter Aid Program," and couldn't help thinking that the autobahns were something great. Did as the Romans did. And made no protest, so long as it didn't concern their own skins.

Then, when it really did concern their own skins, it was too late for protest. His mother was killed by a bomb fragment shortly before the end of the war. "A stray bomb," said his father, as if he had to assure Andreas that the allies had not expressly singled out the Silesian miller's daughter as a target.

His father died of cancer a few years later. He cried a lot in his final days; even, for the very first time, spoke a lot about God; and was unbearable to everyone around him, especially the nurses, whom he offended with his well-aimed nastiness and monopolized with his never-ending demands. Only at Susanne, his rich, beautiful, Jewish daughter-in-law, did he ever smile. "You're kind, my child, you'll look after Andreas." "After both of you." "For me, there's no longer any need…." Brought out in a series of gasps, but with a ravenous will to live in eyes that were becoming clouded. Wasn't anyone going to contradict him? "…but for Andreas. He needs you. Unfit for life." A triumphant look, the judgment was final.

Long and terrible death throes. He gurgled half the night. Toward morning his breathing became shallow, then finally he lay there without moving, mouth open.

"He's gotten through it," whispered Susanne, weeping, and pressed the dead man's eyes closed. "Don't you want to say 'Our Father' or something like that? I don't know your prayers."

Andreas didn't want to.

"You're heartless. After all, he was your father."

He laughed at the "after all." She looked at him with a horrified expression. "How can you? In the presence of death."

Irritated by his silence, she said carelessly, "You've never had anything to do with death. For us in the camp, laughter was a thing of the past. Mountains of corpses."

"Including the twenty-four you have on your conscience?"

He had never mentioned it. She'd probably been under the impression he didn't know the story. She paled, except for her nose, which was reddened from crying.

"What's that supposed to mean? I think it's in bad taste for you to start on that right now. You can't really believe I'm responsible for their deaths."

"You betrayed them."

"That's ridiculous! How could I know the Mulders would be so idiotic as to keep that list of addresses in their desk?"

"That doesn't excuse you."

"I was seventeen."

He grabbed her by the hand. "So what if you'd been ten? Did you believe that security man when he said he only wanted to go back for your suitcase? Tell me if you believed him!"

"Ow. You're hurting me! Don't be so crude. Of course I believed him."

"You gave away the addresses. Despite knowing what a rat Pretty Eddy was."

"No. I didn't know. Never heard his name."

She was lying. Every kid in Amsterdam knew his name. A vertical fold formed between her brows. Unmoved amber eyes. The eyes of a goddess who unfeelingly lets herself be mounted by men.

"Did he touch you?"

"He kissed me, if that's what you mean. Of course he kissed me. Or do you think he went back after my things for nothing?"

"You told him where the Mulders lived. People who were risking their lives by hiding you."

"He promised me nothing would happen to them. I can't help it if he didn't keep his promise. It came down to the fact that my life was at stake. I didn't even have a coat with me when he picked me up, no change of clothes, no soap, nothing. A pocket comb and a tiny stump of lipstick. He said my chances of making it through would be much better if I could pretty myself up a little. And he was right."

"And why didn't you stay home?"

"Do you think anyone could stand that at seventeen? Sitting around in a musty middle-class room without seeing a single person? And besides, other people weren't able to stand it, either."

He felt like hitting her. But he didn't. She gave a supercilious smile, took him gently by the hand, and led him out.

It was high time. Lack of oxygen, the sweetish smell of sweat, the sunken doll in the bed. Ready to throw up.

For all his experience with death, he'd had very little with dead bodies. The first one he'd weighted down with rocks and furtively thrown into a canal one night. His father's was only the second one he'd seen.

And it was causing a lot more fuss. Susanne forced him to put on a black tie and go to the registry office, cemetery, undertaker, florist, and newspaper. "You have to learn about these things," she said when he protested, "It's just not right for a grown man to behave this way."

Things weren't difficult at the registry office or the cemetery. Two counters for death notices: one for A-L, the other for M-Z. They had a burial plot, his mother was lying in it already. Picking out a coffin took some deliberation. He walked back and forth between simple boxes and ostentatious monstrosities trimmed with silver. Couldn't decide. Do you really need one anyway? How simple the canal was.

"Cremation?" asked the owner of the establishment, a man still young, wearing the professional garb of dark suit and mournful expression. "In that case a rental coffin would suffice."

"No. No fire." An impression you couldn't get rid of—that fire hurts. "That one there."

"That is our simplest model. The deceased was of academic rank."

Such carefully chosen words, the prepositional phrase.

"The Jews put their dead in simple wooden boxes."

"I didn't know… Naturally there is no objection to that."

Susanne called up later and ordered a different one. She couldn't change the death notice. Within the black border stood the name of his father. Nothing else.

"You're horrible," said Susanne, "absolutely impossible. A poet ought to be able to think up something."

"I'm not a poet of death notices."

But of death. Of the never-ending song of mourning. The words get lost on their way from head to paper.

The boy had both hoops now. Whirled them skillfully around his body. The girl watched, a finger in her mouth, her eyes full of tears. Suddenly she looked at Andreas, reproachfully, as if he'd taken the hoop away from her.

He shrank back from this reproach, which wounded him in spite of its unjustness, and walked to his car. Now he had to decide where he wanted to go.

Faraway places no longer held any attraction. Staying here was even more impossible. He pulled out slowly. To the right, to the left? Somewhere unfamiliar? No. To the most familiar place of all, back to the place where the beginning and end were: to Amsterdam.

Chapter 2

I n the hanging display case beside the door, the picture of a
baby—blond, brighteyed, laughing. Still above it, in gold letters,
that horrendous sentence: "Modern Artphotos Sabine Lisser."

Go up? Not go up? Not go up. Sabine's shrill voice was unbearable. A file against glass. (The comparison was Daniel's.) Where else
to go?

Once around the block. Down Euterpestraat, which was now
called Gerrit-van-der-Veenstraat: the Dutch no longer wanted to
hear the name of the muse that had been degraded to a Gestapo symbol ("I have to report to Euterpestraat"—good reason to drop out of
sight, submerge, or else take your own life); Albrecht-Dürerstraat,
Cliostraat, back to Beethovenstraat. In front of Sabine's display case
again. When he'd seen it for the first time, there had been a baby picture in it as well. ("Babies are sweet," Sabine had said, "and make people who pass by want to have their pictures taken, too. Even artists
have to know a little about advertising.") Not a blond, blue-eyed one,
but a dark-haired one, with heavy lids. But he'd been laughing,
too. The babies in Sabine's display were all laughing. The one from
back then would be more than twenty now. Should have been. One
chance in six million that he was still alive.

Back then, that was 1942. Up until that time he'd been able to
work at home almost undisturbed. Even though, at the examination,
he'd come up against a draft board physician who had it in for intel-
lectuals with nervous hearts and listed him 1A. But he didn't want to
be a soldier. Never before had he not wanted something with such
vehemence. Enormous concentration on not-wanting-to. At the
door of the examining room, he'd collapsed.

Under the tutelage of a physician friend, he succeeded in proving that he should be rejected and didn't need to put on a uniform. Influential friends found a place for him on a newspaper that was satisfied with occasional literary contributions but nevertheless listed him as a features editor and obtained his deferment. Then, after a change of management, he was informed that he could be kept on only at full time status and sent to Amsterdam as a reporter.

On an August day already permeated by fall, he arrived and moved into a room on Beethovenstraat that had been rented in advance from a pensioned colonial official.

Going up the stairs, he encountered a woman with a yellow Star of David on her breast. When he politely said, "Good day," she turned her head away.

Did they have to do that? He considered anything possible. (Just think what he was still imagining as "anything" in those days!) At any rate, he made a note to speak to her next time, just to let her know what he thought about it all.

In a minute, he'd forgotten her. The room into which he was led by the housekeeper—Mejuffrouw van Lier, squinting over nickel-rimmed glasses, gigantic bosom—was full of South Sea bric-a-brac.

"May I put those things away?"

"Mijnheer would not want that." In almost perfect, even if heavily accented, German.

"I would like to ask Mijnheer myself."

"That's not possible. Mijnheer is ill."

Without a further word, she walked out.

Living with wicker baskets, woven tapestries, even with arrows and spears might be tolerable; but living with two grinning masks, tourist souvenirs from Indonesia, was impossible. He took them from the wall and put them, face down, into one of the baskets. Unpacked his suitcase. Put his typewriter on the little round table, shoved a piece of cardboard under one leg, and started to work. Every hour without working seemed lost. Dying lay in the air, no time to lose, tomorrow it could be your turn, there's still so much to say, the novel's barely half finished. A novel for the dresser drawer, not much call for that style or sentiment. But the war has to be over sometime, you'll be able to speak out again, be a voice again. Until then, keep at it, keep telling the story of Sebastian L., the painter, the forger who loses his own style, because he slips into that of others out of hunger for money, for life.

Not until late in the evening did he go out again. In the moonlight he now noticed what he'd missed previously: a display case of photographs downstairs on the side of the building. A plump, glowingly healthy baby, with heavy, semitic eyelids that cast a melancholy shadow even over the most unrestrained cheerfulness, was laughing happily at a world that did not wish him well. When he thought about the Star of David on the woman on the stairs, he felt a tightening in his throat.

He felt the salty breeze caressing his face, smelled the seaweed, and heard the waves beating against the ship's hull. At the bow hovered Nike, the headless and armless goddess of victory, flying toward the island that lay before them in the dark blueness. Every day he traveled over from Mykonos to the red poppy, the slender lions, the dried-up bowl of the sacred lake, where Apollo had come into the world. Delos, place without death. No one was permitted to die there, no one to be born to the succession of the divine twins. A place of refuge from death on horseback; when he sat among the tiers of the theater and looked out over the sea and islands, he was without fear and certain of his place in the world.

He put his head back and scrutinized the stars. Thanks to the blackout, you could see them in the middle of this big city. *Pour quelque chose malheur est bon*, the French say. He recognized the big dipper, drew a line to the north star, even found the W of Cassiopeia. You ought to take up astronomy. So much you ought to do.

Only as he went on walking did it strike him that he was alone on the street. A big city at night. A warm summer night, a little after ten: he'd heard of the sober life of the Dutch, but this was really going too far. They ought to be drummed out of their houses; he felt like yelling and carrying on, like frightening women, and burying his head in white-skinned breasts, in the pungent smell of pubic hair. Saskia, Hendrickje, Helena, dark eyes and blond hair, behind dark windows they were lying with men.

His heart pounded in his throat. Maybe they weren't doing that at all, maybe they were standing there, waiting, with rifles at the ready, hunters in their shooting stands, turned into killers by patriotic fervor.

He started to run, on tiptoe, so as not to attract attention to himself with the noise, but even the soft tapping sounded loud to his ears.

Two shadows detached themselves from a house. He saw them too late, ran into them, smelled leather. Two blue flashlight beams blinded him.

"Your papers."

He pulled out his passport, the press card.

"So how long y'been here?" A good-natured Bavarian voice.

"Just got here today."

"So that's it," said the second one, then added, with a North-German accent, "Get yourself home as fast as you can. We don't feel like fishing another German out of the *gracht* in the morning."

He was not accustomed to following orders, wanted to protest, swallowed the wrong way, coughed, his lungs hurt, this climate, sea-level, pressure too high compared to Munich.

The Bavarian thumped him on the back and gave him the fatherly advice that he really ought to be in bed with that cold.

He mumbled, "Thanks," did an about-face, and took the shortest way home—or, at least, the one he thought was the shortest, because he soon realized he'd lost his way. The smell of stagnant water, gleaming darkly; he was pretty sure he hadn't come by there earlier.

They'll throw me in, tomorrow morning another German will be missing. An enemy, I'm an enemy, one of *them*, more than I was when I lived in Munich, a member of the occupying power, doesn't matter whether I want to occupy or not, no one's going to ask me about my sentiments before they shove me into the canal.

It was completely dark now. Clouds obscured the moon, a few searchlights probed the sky.

And the silence. It's only supposed to be this quiet out in the woods and meadows; in the city it's spooky, a symptom of illness. He was purposely noisy now, stamping his feet and muttering to himself, but as soon as he stopped to get his bearings, the silence was there again, making the labyrinth, from which he'd never emerge, even more confusing.

Then the moon reappeared from behind the clouds and it was easier to walk. He turned down a street in which he could make out trolley tracks. The trolley ran through Beethovenstraat. But there wasn't enough light to read the street signs.

Finally he heard steps and a man appeared. It was a German soldier, who jumped when Andreas spoke—probably he was afraid of the canal, too—but who politely provided the information that this was Beethovenstraat and walked on after bidding him good night.

Now it was easy to find the building with the hanging display case. He shivered, felt feverish, groped his way up the dark stairway, unlocked the apartment door, continued to feel his way along the dark corridor, didn't know which was the right door, finally decided to open one, and was standing in his own room.

He wanted to buy a lamp. Tomorrow, first thing. With teeth chattering he undressed, fell into bed exhausted, and immediately went to sleep.

Dreamed of noises. Short, quick commands, the barking of dogs, the muted buzzing of many voices, a woman's uncontrollable crying, a drawn-out scream consisting of a single tone that was finally transformed into sobbing, trolleys starting up, their bumpy, echoing rolling.

He awakened sluggishly, with the feeling that he'd actually experienced what he had only dreamed. Mejuffrouw van Lier brought his breakfast on a silver tray with a white lace cover, looked at him mockingly, squinting over her nickel-rimmed glasses, and asked whether he'd slept well.

"Very well, thank you."

"I'm glad."

Obvious sarcasm. As she was about to go, he asked quickly, "Why aren't there any people on the streets at night?"

"We are forbidden, until further notice, to go out after eight o'clock. As a German, *you* can, of course. But then you know what's going on."

He didn't know, hadn't any idea what she meant. Who was playing with whom? What sort of goings-on were the Dutch not supposed to see? Germans being thrown into the canal?

Before he could even ask her, she was, with an agility astonishing for her bulk, already out of the room.

He talked himself into thinking he wasn't bothered by her unfriendliness. After breakfast, he started to write. Worked the whole day, with one short pause during which he ate lunch in a neighborhood restaurant. Writing was the most important thing, more important than the war, which had never penetrated completely into his consciousness. He wouldn't have known what answer to give if someone had asked what war was, except to say it was colossal, gray desolation, in which life fell into disorder. But he needed an ordered life; life and writing were identical. The place didn't matter as long as he could be alone. Not even the South Sea bric-a-brac disturbed him. The sarcastic smile of that van Lier woman diminished to the annoyance level of a buzzing fly. His dreams sank into the nothingness from which they'd come.

It was late when he stopped. Since he didn't feel like wandering through the empty streets again, he went to the window and took a deep breath of air. A strong wind was blowing, the trees were rustling, and again he was aware of the sea, faraway places; resolving to go to the beach as soon as possible, he closed the window. The curtains were clammy. A difficult, exhausting climate; done in, with heavy legs, he got into bed to read, as he was accustomed to, for two or three hours. As a farewell gift, a friend had slipped him Mann's *Lotte in Weimar* disguised behind the dust jacket of a novel by Blunck, the president of the Reich Writers' League. He read with fascination, but after just a few pages, put it aside in the middle of a sentence and, already drifting off to sleep, was barely able to summon up the energy to put out the light.

In the middle of the night he sat up screaming. There they were again: the noises, the short, quick commands, the dogs barking, the muted buzzing of voices. But no crying, no scream.

He wanted to go to the window, was unable to, lay there as if paralyzed, his pajamas sticking to his skin. The trolleys started up, the rolling died away, the footsteps became more distant; then it was quiet.

He looked at the clock: a quarter after two. He tried to read, to take refuge in Weimar, in that world of admiring irony, but the irony was drowned out by the rolling of trolleys, the book fell to the floor, and he lay there half asleep until the van Lier woman came with his breakfast and asked sarcastically, "Did you sleep well?"

"Very well," he said obstinately and stared at her mighty bosom, which seemed ready made for putting your head against it and having a good cry.

It was Saturday, a beautiful, tempting day. He stayed home without working, without even getting dressed, lounged around the room in his pajamas, looked out the window, read a few lines, smoked, started a letter to his mother, tore it up because it sounded too dreary, started again and finished it this time, employing for her benefit his well-practiced art of saying little with many sentences; slipped into his bathrobe to go to the toilet, and met, in the hallway, a pretty woman in a flowered summer dress, a pert little flowered hat on her blond head. She was an uncommon splash of color with violet-blue eyes and she nodded to him langorously, encouragingly. He nodded back, she said, "See you again," and vanished into a room. From inside came voices; she laughed, a man coughed. That had to be the colonial official.

Above the wash basin hung a small mirror. He looked into it and decided the violet-eyed woman wasn't very choosy. Stringy blond hair, sunken, unshaved cheeks, circles under his eyes, and deep creases around his mouth—the face of a sick man or a drunkard.

Back to the room that was foreign, uncomfortable; the two masks were still lying in the basket, a mute protest against that van Lier person.

He lay down on the sofa and waited, waited the whole day, with his heart pounding, trembling with horror and desire, just as he'd waited at death's corner when he was a little boy. In between he nodded off, but slept only lightly for fear of missing things. He was wide awake the rest of the night, standing at the window, staring out at the empty street, the dark houses, the trees, the black sky; but nothing came. Not a sound was to be heard other than the rustling of the wind, which blew incessantly. *Enormous wind, billowing sails, ancient tempest from the sea.*

Chapter 3

THE clock struck five. Now it was no longer out of the question for Sabine to come downstairs. She did her shopping about this time—Jews had been allowed to enter stores only between three and five. After the war she'd said, "I swear by the memory of my dear, departed parents never in my lifetime to go shopping again between three and five." She was tough enough to keep that vow.

He didn't want to meet her. Looked over at the other side of the street, where once there'd been a small hotel. The sign was still hanging there, so he went over and rang the bell.

The proprietor, a middle-aged queer, led him up the steep stairway and opened up a shabby room. "The bed is wide enough, you can…"—pause for effect, with a searching look—"bring a little friend with you."

In the doorway he turned around. "It would be quite charming…" At the impatient gesture, he disappeared immediately and Andreas never found out what would have been charming.

In the front, the room looked out on Beethovenstraat. The same trees, the same houses. Even the trolley cars were still there. They went south filled to the brim, came back to town empty. Their rolling was drowned out by other noises. He listened avidly.

As usual, the wind was blowing. He leaned far out, hoping to catch the smell of the ocean. But it smelled of automobile exhaust fumes instead.

Behind Sabine's window the floodlights were turned on. She was still working, spending a lot of time and energy—honestly convinced that she was producing art—using highlights and deep shadows to make the average face of a Mijnheer or Mevrouw look significant.

One floor below, his own former window. It reflected the building opposite, probably reflected him, too, without his being able to
recognize himself. Nevertheless, the thought amused him. In hopes
of seeing himself anyway, he waved his arms and jumped up and down.
Nothing moved over there. Then he hit upon the idea of getting
his shaving mirror from his suitcase. Held it in the sun. As he tilted it
back and forth, he saw a spot of light moving in his old window. He
tilted the mirror in a definite rhythm, the light on the other side of
the street followed suit. Then he telegraphed the same words over and
over again in a kind of Morse code: *ancient tempest, swell the sails.*

And laughed. The sentence pleased him.

It was not a new sentence. He'd sung it to himself, on a Sunday,
on a deserted beach. Collecting shells, but not those spiral ones that
gave off sound—finding one of them anywhere on the shore had
long ago turned out to be just as impossible as it was desirable, because
such perfection just couldn't exist; and in fact, around here there were
just shallow, gray—or at best pinkish—shimmering scallops. For two
hours he walked across the hard sand, on the lookout for ships, discovered three traveling close behind one another, far away; came
home sleepy from the wind and worked.

After a quiet, dreamless night, he reported to the local command
post, a chore he'd been dreading ever since the trip was over and
which he'd put off as long as possible; but everything worked out
well. He even got to speak with a very amiable adjutant of about his
own age, who, in the course of the conversation, said "we intellectu-
als" and let it be known how glad he was to have *this* post.

With the visit behind him, he took a look at the city. That was part
of his job: he was supposed to file—in addition to reports of actual
events—two or three essays per week, whose topics were left up to
him; it just had to be clear that, where Holland was concerned, it
was a brother country that loved the Germans and the germanic
way of life. (He didn't have to worry about politics—that was the

responsibility of a colleague in the Hague.)

He liked Amsterdam, hadn't expected to—in the south, people were quick to deny any sense of beauty in the north. The basic city plan was clear and intelligent. From the harbor, canals extended in ever-larger concentric circles around the inner city. Of course, this sensible plan had been destroyed at the turn of the century when they built the rail lines and station, separating the city from the harbor. He had trouble even finding the waterfront; when he finally reached it through a tunnel that ran under the railroad tracks, he was disappointed. Idle cranes reared up into the sky and, aside from ferries to the opposite shore, there were only a few river barges in the dirty water.

He took the trolley home, endured the hostile looks when he requested his ticket in German (but made up his mind to learn Dutch as quickly as possible), and had the whole afternoon for work. Went to bed early, still not acclimatized, dead tired again, and with a slight headache.

In a deep sleep, his heart jumped—the noises! This time he didn't scream, but snapped the light on, looked at the clock: exactly 2 a.m. He put out the light, ran to the window and tore it open. Below him were four trolley cars, each with a trailer, and behind them a dark mass was moving—it had to be several hundred people, their faces pale in the bluish beams of flashlights held by boys with white armbands. On the flanks stood a few men in uniform (soldiers? police?) with big police dogs on short leashes.

Muted, terse commands: "Hurry up, hurry up, faster. Car one, one-A, two, two-A, three." The boys with the armbands were dragging suitcases, rucksacks, helping old people. A child blubbered; a woman gave him a slap and yelled, "Don't be so naughty."

They were pushing their way into the cars in a terrible hurry, like clucking chickens running to the feed pot, pushing each other away with their elbows, afraid of not getting to go along, stumbling over the running boards; a man fell, the others climbed up over him, couldn't wait to get in and grab a seat to make themselves comfortable. The dogs jumped at them again and again, checked by their masters with a light slap of the leash.

When they'd all climbed in, in an amazingly short time, a flashlight was swung and the trolleys rolled away; only the uniformed men and the boys with armbands stayed behind, standing there in two distinct groups. Eventually they walked away in different directions without saying goodnight.

The street was empty, the wind blew. After a long time, a car drove by.

He stood with his hands clenching the windowsill until the damp coolness brought on a chill; then he went back into the middle of the room, sat down at the small round table on which the typewriter was still standing open, pushed it aside, laid his head on the tabletop, and said, "Things have gone that far. I've gone crazy."

The fear of old ghosts: tainted on both sides—a brother of his father's was fading away in an insane asylum, a sister of his mother's had taken her own life during a fit of postmenopausal depression. His sensitive artist's nerves, overly reactive even as a child, his father's verdict: unfit for life.

He laughed, cried, wanted to see a doctor, and had to force himself not to go running off to find one right then and there, in the middle of the night.

Trolleys were traveling around in his head, he was hovering high above the earth in a balloon, a gigantic bluish phosphorescent globe, he was sitting at a table, there was a white paper in front of him, he began to cover it with symbols, his mother asked what he was doing and he answered, "I'm writing *The Odyssey*."

From time to time, a glance at the clock. He'd made up his mind not to leave the apartment before eight o'clock; but by seven thirty, things were beyond control. Without a word, he left the van Lier woman standing there as she came from the kitchen with his break-fast tray. So what if she thought he was crazy? He was!

Right in the next street he found a sign on a single-family house: Dr. Max Rosenbusch, *zenuw arts.* (He knew from looking it up in the dictionary that "zenuwen" meant "nerves" and an "arts" was a doctor.)

He rang the bell, but no one answered. He hammered violently on the door with his fists. It was suddenly opened without his having heard a single footstep. On the threshold stood a woman, her face distorted.

A lunatic, he thought, terrified, the doctor's running a private lunatic asylum. He'll keep me here.

He had already half turned to run away when she choked out, "What do you want?"

"To talk to the doctor."

"Why?" So softly he could barely make it out.

"Why would anyone want to talk to a doctor? Because I need one."

She broke out in hysterical laughter: "You're a patient?"

"What else ?"

Again quite softly: "You're not from the Gestapo?"

So she is crazy. Persecution complex.

"Is that what I look like?" he asked softly.

"No. But how is a person supposed to know when someone rings the bell so early and starts pounding on the door?"

It slowly dawned on him how improperly he'd been acting.

"Shall I come back later?"

"No. You should not come back at all. My husband cannot treat you. He is a Jew."

"So?"

"He is not permitted to."

"You can't turn me away."

"I must," she said emphatically, no longer sounding like a crazy woman. "Please leave."

"Would you say the same thing if an injured person came to you? Somebody who was bleeding to death?"

"I don't know. Probably. But anyway, you're not bleeding."

"Just assume that I am."

"A few more minutes wouldn't matter. One of my husband's colleagues lives here on this street, Dr. van Lockeren-Campagne. A very good physician."

"I don't want to go to anyone whose name is Lockeren-Compagne."

"Don't be childish."

"I need a doctor who speaks German."

"Herr van Lockeren-Campagne speaks German. All Dutch physicians..." She hesitated. "Almost all. With few exceptions, one of which is my husband."

"But you're German. And you're telling me the doctor doesn't speak German?"

She nodded. Blushed as well. She was transformed by the lie into an attractive woman who once upon a time must have been beautiful.

"Then I'm sorry," he said and was about to go.

At that moment a seventeen- or eighteen-year-old boy appeared at her side, squinted because of the dazzling light, and looked quizzically from the stranger to his mother. She smiled at him, then said, "It's all right," at which he walked by them with a polite greeting. They both watched him go, for a long while; Andreas's feeling of confusion returned.

This boy, who looked like an Arab lad of unimaginable beauty, whose melancholy, animal eyes had gazed at him fearfully and haughtily—the enemy whom one fears and despises at the same time—this Jewish boy swinging his bookbag and walking away as lithely as if he were going off on a hunt in the forest primeval and not, as was likely, to school—this boy was Andreas himself. His leaving pained

Andreas, it was as if he were being torn in two. Finally, good upbringing functioned again, and Andreas said, putting an end to the episode, "Please forgive me."

Whether he really looked so poorly that the doctor's wife believed medical help was necessary, or whether she'd noticed how he was struck by the boy, she now stepped a little to one side and whispered, "Perhaps…"

As Andreas was still hesitating, a man's voice called from inside (in German, naturally), "Just what is going on out there, Edith?"

"It's a patient."

"Why doesn't he come in?"

She turned her head to the rear. "He's not a Jew."

"If it doesn't bother him, it certainly doesn't bother me."

Then she stepped aside. The doctor was standing in the vestibule: average height, stocky, with round shoulders. An old Jew. An oriental prince. With a small, plump hand (nails clean and manicured) he amicably showed his visitor into the consulting room. No white walls here, no apparatus or instruments; it was the study of a real gentleman, very cultivated, almost luxurious, floor-to-ceiling bookshelves along two walls, a ponderous desk in the middle, a sofa off to one side. How good it would have been to lie down on it, but he was motioned toward a chair. In order to see the doctor sitting behind the desk, he had to turn his head; if he looked straight ahead, he saw a painting that he recognized as a Klee—green branches, with yellow birds sitting on twigs, hanging upside-down, standing on their heads, and flying without spreading their wings. Above them hovered an orange crescent moon. The sight was wonderfully calming, and almost put him in a cheerful mood.

He was allowed to speak, could speak. Described his life briefly. There was little enough to tell since he limited himself to the superficial features, which he did in order not to drown the doctor with a violent flood of images. Mentioned his heredity, the uncle and aunt, those ghosts, and then launched into the full details of the bad dreams from the previous night.

The doctor, slouched behind the desk, listened to him without interrupting, asking questions, or making notes. When the story was over, he laughed softly.

"You are not having hallucinations, and you are not crazy. Just unlucky that they assigned you that particular room and that you decided to come to a Jew for help. Of course, my Christian colleagues would tell you the same thing, but I'm afraid it will sound somewhat different, coming from me. Well, listen. Every night with the exception of Saturday and Sunday—even the devil wants his weekends off—four hundred Jews, men, women, and children, are taken from their homes, loaded into streetcars, taken to the railroad station, and sent from there to a Dutch transit camp. Sometimes according to the alphabet, sometimes according to street, profession, or membership in an organization—it varies. They're inventive, not in any hurry, because when they're finally finished here and Holland's hundred thousand Jews have been transported, they'll be facing duty at the front. There are even reprieves, which are granted when they bring in four hundred and twenty or four hundred and thirty—then they let twenty or thirty go again. Because it has to be four hundred, not one more or one less. They stress order and can afford to act magnanimously in this cat-and-mouse game, but whoever is allowed to go home today will be back again tomorrow. In the end the cat always wins. All those being deported, even children and old people, receive a notice on which it says that they have to join the work brigades in Germany and may take along a rucksack or suitcase, as well as two wool blankets. Their house keys are to be turned in, their furniture is taken away after a few days by an institution called the Household Goods Depot and sent to Germany as a donation from the Dutch people. From the transit camp, a train leaves each week for the east carrying a thousand people. The east—words that allow one to imagine almost anything. Hannover is the east, or Berlin, or Breslau, or Poland. The east is a concept that signifies nothing, or rather, signifies nothing-ness—destination, death. For seven weeks the deportations have been going on. You can figure out how long it will last: barely two years."

The doctor had spoken without any expenditure of energy, as calmly as if he were reading through a case history. When he was finished, his round shoulders became even rounder; he sagged down even more.

Things got black in front of Andreas's eyes. Not black enough for him to faint, which would have relieved him of the need to say any-thing; it was only enough for a pause to catch his breath. The room was full of fog—fog that assaulted your bronchial tubes, took your breath away. He shook his head. Coughed. Came close to telling the doctor that he didn't believe him, and yet knew that he had to believe him. Tried evasion again by telling himself that even this story was part of his insanity. In the end, however, there was nothing left for him to do but recognize it as reality. "Something has to be done," he said.

"It is too late. Those who are off to America did the right thing. The rest of us were too complacent. Our death sentences have been pronounced and will not be commuted at the last moment. The king's messenger on horseback will not appear. Resistance is hopeless. Besides, to even risk it, we would have to be united, and we are not. Hardly anyone is ready to sacrifice himself, everyone just thinks about saving his own skin."

"Not you. *We* have to do something."

"Don't go poking into the fate of strangers. Just try not to see any-thing. Find yourself another room as quickly as possible. That is the only advice I can give you."

The princely head rose above the fog.

Then Andreas said, "Why are you still sitting here? Why don't you go into hiding?"

"Because I do not wish to endanger others."

"That's pride."

"Call it what you will. My wife and I have had a beautiful life. It is not overly difficult to go away. It's just our boy…"

Their voices died away. Silence tore open the fog.

"Send your boy to me."

A smile as thanks. "Not as easy as you imagine. You live in the home of strangers. Don't even know how long you'll be staying here. Besides, the boy wouldn't even do it."

"Why not?" Obsessed by the thought.

"He would not want to owe his escape to a German. That is unjust, I know. But as a seventeen-year-old condemned to death, he has the right to be unjust."

The fog came in again. Yellow, poisonous smog.

"You can't just send me away like this."

The doctor reconsidered. "If you want to honor me with a favor, there is something I can think of."

Violent headnodding.

"It is not free of danger. Nothing may be taken away from Jewish dwellings. If you do not think the risk too great, take this painting along with you. I am very fond of it. All of us are. It is not a pretty thought that it might just moulder away somewhere in a storeroom for degenerate art. But it means even more to me. In our time, we can no longer reach other people with words. Everything that can be said has long since been said. The single mode of communication that is left to us is the symbol. That picture is a symbol: of joy, of cheerfulness, of calm. It's hanging there so my patients can see it. It has helped many. Now I no longer have patients. Take care of it until after the war. If we should survive, give it back. If not, it belongs to you."

With short, hasty steps he went to the wall and took the painting from its hook.

"I am very grateful to you. Perhaps I can now convince Daniel that there are Germans who are prepared to help us."

Along with the picture, Andreas received the name.

The doctor rummaged around in his desk for paper. Together they wrapped the painting.

"At least write my name down," Andreas requested.

"Even that can be dangerous for you."

When he reacted with an impatient movement, the doctor scribbled the address on a scrap of paper. Put it into his wallet.

"Thank you," Andreas said and hesitated. He thought about the fact that he had mentioned nothing about meeting Daniel. Should he sit down again and say, "Your son and I are one and the same person?" That would be a significant symptom. Perhaps then the doctor would treat him after all and relieve his symptoms. But he wasn't willing to divulge it. "Thank you," he said again, clamped the package under his arm, and left.

Walked into the street and squinted—blinded just as much by the light as Daniel had been.

A tall fellow rose up in front of him, in a shabby raincoat—why a coat in this sun?—with a hangdog face. Barked out a question in Dutch. Andreas shrugged his shoulders.

Do you say *Kannitverstan*? The only Dutch word he'd learned at school. Doubt it really is Dutch. Then, in spite of that: "Kannitverstan."

It had the desired effect. The fellow spoke German (poorly).

"What are you dragging off from the Jew's?"

"Nothing." The stupidest of all possible answers.

"So, that's nothing. Interesting. Come with me."

Silently they trotted along beside one another, through the not-very-busy Beethovenstraat; hangdog-face wasn't in a hurry, he seemed to want to savor the good fortune of having taken a prisoner. The painting was getting heavy.

Slight giddiness, not unpleasant, actually a good feeling: Now they have me, I can do something for the Rosenbusches, it's all right.

What the "doing" was supposed to consist of, he didn't know, he wasn't even imagining anything really dangerous; the adventure was making him more curious than frightened.

Astonishing how many people have on raincoats with not a cloud in the sky, it's just that the wind is blowing. But it's actually cool, probably you shouldn't ever go out without a coat here, they know their climate. Better than too hot—sweating would be unpleasant, that guy might think I was afraid.

They walked through a crowded street at the edge of town, shoved through the torrent of people. As they came into the crowd, dogface grabbed him by the arm. "Let go! I'm not going to run away on you." To his astonishment, he was released. It wouldn't be difficult to disappear in the throng. But the guy was likely to be armed and might even shoot, despite the danger of hitting someone else. So, stay right there. Keep on walking with him.

Women with their shopping bags, young boys on bicycles, old men with a rocking gait like sailors. The beautiful skin of the girls. At a corner a pair of lovers. They're scarcely touching each other, just her hand on his sleeve, unending tenderness. Envy. Have to meet a girl. But probably only a slut would go with a German. You're a leper. What a misfortune to have been born there. Boche. Here they say "*Mof.*" You learn that right away, on the first day. It comes hissing out behind you. From self-confident mouths. They don't underestimate themselves, have few inhibitions. That makes them beautiful, even though they're not beautiful. Uglier than people at home, but freer. Have a more fortunate history. Freedom fighters by tradition. You have to read *The Revolt of the Netherlands* again. And *Egmont*.

A lot of people with the yellow star. A woman fearfully presses her bag in front of it so that only the points are sticking out. But most display it openly, supported by the sympathy of the rest of the people, who make way for them as if the privilege of walking anywhere unhindered were their due.

Ugly shops with crammed displays. Wartime merchandise. Probably not much different in peacetime. In Germany they're displaying ersatz things. Store after store with cheap candy. Must be ruining their teeth. Dog-face has dentures. That van Lier woman, too. No wonder. Next to confectionery, lamps seem to be the most sought-after article. Lower middle-class coziness, pink, yellow, orange silk shades. Furniture, curved, carved, decorated with metal; easy chairs covered in a dirty red; heavy, dark wallpapers on which there are flying birds (no yellow ones), entwined blossoms, brocade patterns giving a false sense of opulence. From the drugstores, the smell of cheap perfume reaches out into the street. A man next to a large, brightly colored hurdy-gurdy playing "O du lieber Augustin." A second one with a brass money-box. He would have given him something, but was afraid that dog-face would grab hold of him again.

It was high time to decide what he was going to say about the painting. But no matter how much he tried to concentrate, nothing occurred to him. He noticed that his forehead felt moist despite the cold. Only now was he beginning to sense that he was in danger and that he couldn't do anything for the Rosenbusches, only harm them. Not only did he have to think up something, he had to think up something they'd believe. An exam where the grades were life or death. The examiners, unknown: were they as crude as his companion, soldiers, torturers? Or civil servants, experienced investigators equipped with all the tricks of the trade? My kingdom for a *story*! But stories don't just fall from the sky, they need time to ripen, and he had no time. They were already close to the inner city; he didn't know where he was being taken, but they could be there any moment. Then he'd have to do some talking. Lies. When had he ever lied? When he'd told the draft board physician about his heart problem? But that was a script that had been provided by a medical man and memorized. When he'd nodded at Mama's statement that he was going to the museum to study the gothic madonnas? But that had been her statement and not his. And often, when he'd said "Yes" to that question asked by girls: "Do you love me?" But that had been the girls' question, not his. He couldn't remember any others. Telling lies had never interested him, and it never entered his mind that you had to master the art of lying to be fit for life.

He felt a poke in his side: "In here."

They entered a dusty guard room. Behind a barrier sat an SS man with the flattened nose of a boxer. The scum is doing the dirty work for us here. On the wall hung a picture of Hitler.

Dog-face spoke Dutch to the other man, who nodded a few times.

"I'm a German."

"Quiet!" bellowed the boxer.

Dog-face ripped the package from under his arm. Their heads edged forward for a closer look. As the painting emerged, the boxer broke into a horse laugh; dog-face joined in after a moment of fright.

The laughter awakened fear. Full realization of how much he was in their power. They could do anything with him (and now "anything" meant something a lot different from before): beat him, torture him, send him to a concentration camp. Scum knows only hate, is blind to symbols.

The boxer tore the painting from its frame. Shredded it out with club-like hands. Then he started to bellow again: "What's this smear supposed to be?"

Andreas bit his lip. There was a roaring in his ears.

"Answer when you're asked a question!"

The bellowing helped him. There was no time to consider whether the story produced by his terrified imagination had even the slightest chance of being believed. Distinctly and slowly, as if he were speaking to children who could hardly talk yet, he said that the picture ("It's not very pretty, I have to admit") had been painted by his younger brother. "He used to go to school with the Jewish boy and lent it to him. When I was leaving for Amsterdam, he asked me to get it back. Which I did today."

Couldn't they read? The painting was signed. How easy it would be to find out that he didn't have a brother named Klee. His eyelid twitched. He didn't dare tremble. And in fact didn't tremble.

Laziness was the loophole one could slip through. They didn't bother to ask for his name.

"Typical that a Jew boy would like such crap," said the boxer. "Birds standing on their heads. An' a orange slice for a moon. Take it outa here. But be quick about it. I don't want to look at it any more. Heil Hitler!"

"Heil Hitler," said Andreas with arm outstretched. In Germany, he'd managed not to say "Heil Hitler" for nine whole years.

Then he rolled up the painting, carried it in one hand and the splintered frame in the other, and didn't look back. At home, he threw the frame away, put the painting up on the wall of his room with thumbtacks.

There was a big tear through the middle. The yellow birds were decapitated and missing their tails. The symbol of joy had been transformed, had become that which it remained from then on: the symbol of destruction.

Chapter 4

WITH breakfast came the newspaper. The number of traffic fatalities had increased by ten percent, in New Zealand (very far away) an infant had been gnawed by rats, in Cuba (also far away, though somewhat closer) seven people had been condemned to death and shot three hours later, in West Germany a former SS Colonel accused of forty thousand murders had been acquitted because of lack of evidence, a passenger plane with seventy-six people on board was missing over Pakistan, the Dutch Foreign Minister had flown to Canada, the President of the Congo to the United States, the American Defense Minister to England, the Austrailian Premier to Japan, the churches were calling for relief work in developing countries: a hundred thousand people are starving every day.

He chewed on a piece of jelly bread. Abject sympathy. A hundred thousand are starving every day. It wouldn't help a bit if he didn't touch the bread. They'd go on starving. Yesterday and today, and tomorrow and the day after tomorrow. A hundred thousand—exactly as many as the murdered Jews of Holland. Three hundred sixty five times a year, including Saturdays and Sundays. Too many to even imagine. Four hundred, that's something you can imagine, you can take in four hundred with one glance when they're pushing into the trolley cars in the beams of blue flashlights. A hundred thousand is a word from mathematics, the stock exchange, statistics. A hundred thousand dead is an abstraction, four hundred are human beings.

Four hundred wandered across the paper like a black shadow when he wanted to write and shattered his composure.

In fifteen years the population of the earth will have doubled. Will two hundred thousand starve daily then? Will the murdered Jews matter then?

They will matter. He still believed that. Still believed in the necessity of bearing witness to their fate.

He got up, washed, dressed slowly, half-heartedly; another stroke with the shaving brush, moistened his face once again with the shaving lotion, tied his shoes over again—when there was absolutely nothing more to be done, he took a black notebook out of his suitcase and sat down at the table which, like all hotel tables, was too low, too small, and wobbly besides. Unscrewed the cap from the fountain pen and began to draw in the air above the paper. That accursed white paper. An embittered battle to take away its whiteness, that simulated innocence behind which it was daring you to try to take possession of it. He shoved the end of the pen into his mouth, played around it with his tongue (just as in kissing) and then bit down. Then stuck the point into his finger until he drew blood. He wiped it across the paper, tore the page from the notebook, crumpled it up, and threw it into the wastebasket. There were times when he let the pen glide over the paper. Spirals appeared, curves that would not end, that bit their own tails and wandered, lost, through the labyrinth that they themselves had just constructed. Sometimes faces grew out of them, caricatures with pouting lips, squat-nosed, above foreheads towered coiffures, hovered gigantic feathered hats; large heads without necks sat on tiny bodies. As soon as a page was full, it flew into the wastepaper basket. He used up whole notebooks that way. But he always found new ones waiting. Susanne ordered them by phone from the best shop in the city.

He even wrote down words. But the mesh of the nets was too coarse to catch the right ones; he tried with the rod, sometimes fished out an impressive word, a beautiful, bulging, iridescent one, and disappointedly let it slide back into the big sea. Because what's a single word anyway? It's like a single column, without relationship, without tension and a single column hardly makes a Roman ruin, it's really nothing at all.

Now and again whole sentences worked out, beginnings of poems, short stories, novels. As soon as he put them down on paper and saw what he'd written in his small, nervous, forward-striving script, it revolted him. He tore the pages out. The wastepaper baskets were overflowing. Susanne telephoned for new supplies.

She gave him a fountain pen for Christmas. Packed in gold paper, with a red silk bow. The best of all possible instruments of torture. Eighteen carat. In the circular it said that a specimen of this model had been dropped from a church tower without being broken. He'd bitten his to pieces within three days. A liveried messenger brought a new one.

He tried the typewriter. In hopes that the interposed technology would act as a liberating medium. In vain. The sheets filled themselves with symbols typed on top of one another, one word gobbled up the next, letters and punctuation marks staggered across the surface.

Out of these possibilities, discovered by accident, grew systematic experiments. Mutation of vowels, transposition of sounds, exact calculations as to how many variations it took before one returned to the point of departure.

And again and again, capitulation: grab one of the books lying on the desk, leaf through quickly, read hurriedly, sometimes dwell at length, fascinated. The wish to find out how the others were doing it.

They had a lot of ways of expressing themselves. Things were implied and lyrically encoded, objectively reported and baroquely adorned; identities were questioned, time and space suspended, crammed together, expanded to the bursting point; horror was portrayed through the absurd. They no longer cried over head- and tail-less birds, but made a principle of them. That's the way to do it! The image of our world. The low point is the time when our star shines most brightly.

Too many forms offered themselves. If he'd decided on one, the next day he found another one he liked better. And none fit.

He couldn't change his style. It belonged to him like part of his body. But his style didn't fit, either.

He had a wildly exaggerated desire to be true, was a fanatic for precision. But he didn't acknowledge any truth that did not begin with four hundred human beings deported in trolley cars. To write about any other subject was impossible. But for this one, there was no word, no symbol, no simile that covered it.

His memory deserted him. He recalled the non-essentials, the important things were gone. Sabine's babbling he could remember word for word, Daniel's voice had died away. An undependable witness. Shouldn't ask him to swear to anything.

He no longer even knew the story of Sebastian L. very clearly, and yet had spent years of his life telling it. He scratched around in the debris that lay over it. Not much was uncovered.

What did Sebastian L. look like? (Unimportant. Perhaps had always been unimportant.) What sort of women did he love? He called one Cherubin. (And her real name?)

Painter of abstract pictures. (Were they really abstract? Not expressionist? Wasn't Beckmann his ideal at that time, rather than Kandinsky?) No matter, whether abstract or expressionist, he was a good painter. A hopeful. Like himself. Has he anticipated his own fate in that of Sebasian L.? He's not a forger.

Even Sebastian L. didn't want to turn to forgery. Only when it was no longer possible for him to go on painting in his own style in Germany did he busy himself with the old masters and produce—just for practice, mind you—a picture of a woman who looked like Saskia. But why did he sell it then?

He showed it to an expert (or a museum director) who considered it genuine and offered him so much for it that he couldn't resist. Wealth aroused greed. Sebastian L. had money and wanted more.

New things turned up. Presumably a van Dyck, a Goya, a Vermeer. Never two by the same painter. Never two in the same city. After each picture, a long interval. Travels, adventures, affairs. The grand life.

Then, one day, when he tried to paint a picture of his own again, he no longer could. His personality was gone, his talent in the devil's hands. It's fairly certain that about this time, the first doubts as to the authenticity of the paintings began to crop up.

How should it go on? Would the painter be arrested? Sent to prison? What sort of ending was planned? The end is always death, but there was probably some intention to let Sebastian L. go on living. Murky, in other words; no decision. Life, but not a happy one, fading away in uncertainty.

Why was he thinking about a shadow that didn't help him get on with things? That revealed nothing to him other than the fact that things couldn't go on that way? For him, the time for telling stories was past. He had an accusation to lodge against his fellow men. Those murderers.

He began to write. A new beginning. It had to work here, where it had happened. Just tell, don't comment. Gather in the noises. The scream of a woman. A command. A child crying. A dog's bark. The rolling of the trolley cars.

His cramped hand hurt. He kept on writing. About the four hundred people who crowded onto the trolleys, who pushed each other aside in order to get on quickly. Instead of faces, bluish masks, and shining stars over their hearts. Standing in their midst, he himself, someone who didn't belong there, with his everyday face and unstarred jacket. Shoving forward, they pressed him to the ground, trampled him. He couldn't breathe. The thread broke. With a curse, he crumpled up the paper and threw it into the wastebasket.

Chapter 5

THEY had to believe him: he hadn't known anything before that first night with the trolleys. It would be difficult to convince them. Nine years of the Third Reich and hadn't noticed anything?

Of course he'd noticed something. Just not the right things, not the truth.

Perhaps he didn't really want to know?

They should quit pestering him with Freud. He'd rather be condemned than talk his way out with such a shabby excuse. Where would he have been able to find the truth?

Hadn't he ever heard names like Oranienburg, Sachsenhausen, Dachau, Buchenwald?

They were put into categories like TB, cancer, syphilis, going blind, becoming deaf, automobile accidents, and airplane crashes—things you know about and are afraid of, but seldom think about; and if you do, then only with the firm conviction that they're not going to happen to you.

Didn't he know anyone who'd been in a concentration camp?

A few, in passing. A gardener's helper who sometimes trimmed the hedge. An Intourist employee, met two or three times at the home of mutual friends. A young Jewish attorney with whom he'd drunk champagne one night during Fasching. Just one closely: the old Jewish Health Commissioner, his parents' family doctor.

Had he seen them again?

The gardener's helper still trimmed the hedge. In answer to questions like how was he doing and whether it had been bad there, you'd like to hear the details, he said, "I'm OK." Clacked away with the shears and stared intently at the branches. The conversation was over.

Nothing could be found out concerning the Intourist man. Just guesses. He could, once released from Dachau, have moved to another city. Or have gone to Russia. Or—but this was difficult to believe and hardly possible—was still in the camp. Was being held there, without an order for his arrest, without a judge's verdict, just because he was an employee of a Russian travel agency. You pushed that thought far away from you. You held on tightly to the illusion that you lived in a country of law and order.

The Jewish attorney had died in Dachau. His parents got the sealed coffin and the death certificate as well: heart attack. They claimed that their son had never noticed anything at all wrong with his heart. Then what did he die of? It was easy to suspect that the dead man, well known to be a relentless seducer, had been murdered by the SS boyfriend of some girl. Personal revenge, you said, and didn't think any further about it.

The Health Commissioner came to say goodbye two days after being relieved of his post. He'd been forced to agree (here he corrected himself: had taken it upon himself) to emigrate within a week. He looked sick, aged. "My gallbladder, you know, it's always given me trouble." That sounded entirely plausible. A lot of Jews had gallbladder trouble, they ate too much and too well.

When they were alone again, his mother shed a few tears. "I don't know what I'd do if I had to leave my house and everything. But probably the idea of a hometown doesn't mean as much to them as it does to us. No power on earth would make me go away voluntarily. The worst part of it is that we'll have to find a new family doctor."

Did he think that was the "worst part of it" as well?

Naturally not. Are his powers of imagination being underestimated?

It was clear to him what an emigre's existence meant. Wandering through unfamiliar cities, alone. Living in grubby boarding houses.

Running from committee to committee. Not being able to drink a cup of coffee because you didn't have the money or, if you did have it, not allowing yourself to, so as to save your assets. Having to sell lightbulbs when you'd been a lawyer, having to take exams when you'd had a professorship. Sitting beside the radio, all day, all night, waiting for news that never came. Throwing oranges at the telephone because no one called. Trembling with fear at the immigration office, worrying about whether you'll be permitted to stay. Begging for a visa at consulates. Lying in bed in a hospital, in a big ward, and dying in a foreign language. Dependent, humiliated, outside the law. And praising all this as freedom and being thankful for it.

And about Germany he didn't know anything? Hadn't he read *Mein Kampf*, the *Völkischer Beobachter*, the *Stürmer*?

Who read that sort of junk? He had more important things to do.

Or listened when they went marching by with their bumzaza and fly the flag high and Heil Hitler and tomorrow the world belongs to us and Jewish blood spurts from the knife?

Everyone was convinced that the world wouldn't belong to them and so you didn't believe the Jewish blood business either.

Or looked? At Jewish crystal, Jewish porcelain, Jewish carpets and tapestries, smashed, kicked to pieces, thrown into the street?

Didn't see it myself, but, over lunch, my tearful Mother described it in detail. (She controlled her tears like a virtuoso, they flowed or stopped, depending on her wishes. Her good technique enabled her to cry and eat simultaneously. And she never cried so hard that things would get stuck in her throat.) "Just a gang," said Father, likewise chewing. *"Be careful, my dear."* In English, for tactical reasons; if the maid walked in, the warning was sometimes given in English, sometimes in French. It didn't matter that Father didn't understand English, he knew what was meant. The maid knew, too. "Y'r right Professor, robbers's what they are, and firebugs." But there she'd overstepped the line. Papa cleared his throat before saying,

"Do not mix in our conversation. You don't know what you're talking about. I have been speaking about an historic event that has no relationship to the present." Nodded with satisfaction. In case she had been trying to provoke him into an incriminating statement, you never know; she'd been rebuffed. She and Father stared at each other full of mistrust. Mistrust everywhere. Uneasiness and hatred.

So he already hated the Nazis at that time?

If you take him at his exact word—no, probably not. Why should he? They let him write and he didn't want anything more.

Just uneasiness, then? From which he drew no conclusions?

What sort of conclusions are to be drawn from uneasiness? You could only protest silently.

Inner emigration?

No. Even then, *that* concept seemed to him just as stupid as it was fraudulent. He'd just decided to stay there.

And why had he stayed?

You have to understand. There were many who expected great things of him, he couldn't disappoint them. We have to stay to prevent even worse things. It became a slogan behind which convenience, cowardice, and even conviction were hidden. He had conviction. Felt obligated by the fame that his first poems had brought him. "A new voice of the highest order," he'd been called. You couldn't run away and let those mutilators of language have a free hand.

So he'd gone on writing as if nothing had changed?

In greater peace than before. He'd been in danger of going commercial, falling for that literary carrying-on with poetry readings in auditoriums and, by candlelight, in the homes of old women who'd kiss him on the forehead. Now the state was promulgating another style. And Johst from the Reich Writers' League was reading in the salons of kissing women.

Did he go on writing while the books were burning?

The flames revealed the murderers' grimaces. Tore open the darkness for brief moments. For the first time, serious consideration of emigrating. But his friends insisted, you must stay, and so he stayed. Withdrew, lived in a cave, by artificial light, screened off from the outside world, and wrote. A novella, poems. Scarcely any difference between the lyric poetry and the prose. Many readers thought they found opposition to the regime in a few lines. They read more secrets into them than were there. When words like occident, secret, light, darkness, spirit, desperation turned up, they smelled revolt. But he wasn't a fighter. He said no just as little as he said yes. At least until he began to tell the story of Sebastian L.

How had he come to that?

The first appearance of the artist-figure at the exhibition of degenerate art. Still quite indistinct, scarcely outlined. Developed out of indignation. What was hanging on those walls in Germany for the last time, specifically for the purpose of being ridiculed and despised, was not just some artistic tendency that anyone was free to reject; it was a compendium of the art of our time.

Was it then he'd finally decided on "No"?

Even if only for himself. He knew that there was no possibility of publication. He withdrew into his cave with Sebastian L., his companion for the coming years.

What else could he have done? He was a pacifist. The greatest commandment: thou shalt not kill. The childish belief that others wouldn't kill either. They had to believe him: before the trolleys he hadn't understood a thing about the essence of fascism. That was his crime.

Chapter 6

THE photographer was a ridiculously unimportant secondary figure. Who cared whether she was still alive? Who cared whether, at this very moment, she was crossing the street under his window with her slightly waddling gait? She had played her role, had returned to her solitary existence, and without a doubt continued to think of her spotlights as a life-giving constellation. But it was still not clear whether she'd actually started the trouble by showing up. Would he have been able to prevent her from coming if he hadn't been in the Hague with the violet-eyed woman on that exact day? If he hadn't played the role of her rescuer during the first roundup? Would Daniel have stayed home if it hadn't been for her constantly irritating presence? Why, why? Why was Sabine alive and why was Daniel dead?

When he met her on the stairs for the second time, he already knew from the van Lier woman that she was a photographer. She was dragging a large suitcase downstairs. The yellow star was carelessly sewed down just at two corners. It annoyed him, he couldn't tolerate slovenliness and thought the Jews should summon up some dignity in the face of their humiliation.

Well, it really didn't concern him. But since he'd already made up his mind to, and also because he now knew she was doing something forbidden and what repercussions it could have for her, he stopped, greeted her politely (perhaps even exaggeratedly), and asked whether he could help her take the suitcase somewhere.

Her pudding-face exploded with astonishment. Her mouth tore open. Like a carp gasping for air. At the same time she clutched the bag anxiously, as if she were afraid it was going to be stolen from her. And turned her head toward the wall.

He noticed angrily that he was blushing, mumbled—aware of the unjustness—"Stupid cow," and went into his room in a bad mood to get down to the daily nuisance of producing an article. It was costing him significantly more trouble than he'd thought it would in the beginning. His limitations as a journalist were considerable. Added to that was his revulsion toward the things he was supposed to say.

In large print, he wrote across the sheet: In the name of the German people murder is being committed. Crumpled up the page and threw it into the basket. (Perhaps back then he was making, for the very first time, the gesture in which all of his writing was later to end.) Then he fed a new sheet into the machine, worked himself down to the level of his correspondence with Mama, and typed trivialities about the Dutch landscape, Dutch personalities, and German theater evenings. (The curfew had been lifted—for the Dutch, not for the Jews—at that point, evening performances were being given, the culture-machine of the occupying power was running in high gear, impeded only by a conspicuous boycott on the part of the Dutch.) Boring sophomoric essays. The newspaper accepted them without praise or censure; they didn't seem accustomed to anything better.

In his notebook, a record of those nights was being kept in secret code. The thought of being a witness was becoming an idee fixe. He never asked himself whether others couldn't give testimony, too. It was *his* duty, behind which receded everything he'd wanted to do up until now.

From day to day, the figure of Sebastian L. became less well defined, his problems lost validity, new ones presented themselves. Forgers climbed higher on the social scale, forgers of identity papers, official stamps, releases for prisoners, birth certificates, certificates of baptism, and proof of ancestry. The forger of art had every chance of becoming a hero of the resistance. Serious consideration of changing the concept. He began to sense the difficulties of writing a novel based on certain norms of social coexistence at a time when the norms had been suspended.

Weeks of solitary life. He spoke to no one other than the house-keeper, didn't write any letters and didn't get any. Except for the anx-ious cries of his mother that fluttered punctually onto his table once a week. Was he taking care not to get his feet wet, was his wash being done properly, was he eating sensibly, and above all was he avoiding foolish encounters with women? Would he please remember at all times that he was in a hostile foreign country?

He couldn't stand other people. Even the few minutes with that van Lier woman brought on vertigo, nausea, headaches. It seemed as if she could sense that; she knocked, came in, put the tray on the table, and left without a word. When a message or a question was unavoidable, she gave it briefly, limited it to the facts, and he answered the same way.

Until one evening she was standing in his room without knock-ing. Her bosom heaved. She was sputtering with excitement.

"Now they're in our street. Going from house to house and tak-ing the Jews with them."

He looked at her silently. What was he supposed to say?

"Your countrymen," she hissed without constraint. "Those pigs."

The fact that he nodded did not mollify her, but made her even more indignant. Under her angry gaze, he didn't even dare wipe off the saliva droplets she'd spit onto his hand. She lifted her arms in lamentation and said ponderously, "Poor Lisser."

He trembled. The thought that that unattractive person, who wouldn't even talk to him, was going to be taken away was more ago-nizing than if it had been any of the three hundred ninety-nine oth-ers. Was he too unimaginative to envision the pain of people he didn't know? Like his mother, who refused to eat a chicken she'd seen alive? That was *her* chicken; at that moment, Sabine Lisser became *his* Jew.

The chair fell over as he jumped up and ran out of the room. "Are you going to denounce me?" screamed the van Lier woman behind him.

He took the steps three at a time—every second could be critical. Panting, he arrived upstairs and rang the bell. The Lisser woman opened the door immediately. She must have been standing behind it, dressed to go out, in a dark blue suit with a veiled hat and white gloves. Over her shoulder hung a knapsack, beside her stood a suitcase with the top strapped shut.

An uncomprehending, terrified gaze from big, cow eyes. A sacrificial animal with veiled hat.

"Come."

She shook her head violently. The veil fluttered.

"Come on!"

"Where?"

"To my place. Quickly, before they're here."

"You're crazy."

He heard someone come into the building down below, took the suitcase, grabbed the woman by the wrist and dragged her along down the stairs.

"No, no, no!" Like a contrary child she resisted with her entire body, stumbled, and started to cry.

Loud, totally inconsiderate person. As far as either of them knew, the secret police could already be downstairs.

Finally he succeeded in dragging her into his room, where the van Lier woman was still standing, her face bright red.

"Oh," she said. "Well, alright."

Sabine Lisser sat down. "You hurt me." All complaints and feeling sorry for herself.

The housekeeper went to the door. "I'll see whether the Mofs have gone up to your place. But stop bawling. It's disgraceful."

Sabine lit up a cigarette. She smoked hastily. The ashes fell on the floor.

Without taking the cigarette out of her mouth she asked, "What made you do that?"

He shrugged his shoulders. The question was not unjustified. What made him do that? But he had to answer her, so he said, "I didn't want you to be taken away."

"Don't understand. You're still a Mof."

Again this person was making him blush.

"Why me?" she bored away. "You don't even know me."

He pushed an ashtray toward her. The ashes kept on falling to the floor.

Sloppy dame. Awful. Fingers yellowed from smoking. But maybe from the darkroom. Unjust again. But why her? Perhaps a mother with several children is being taken away right now. Or a Nobel Laureate. Or a young bride. Or—no, not Daniel. Not Daniel. Not that.

Why is she the one? Why her? The evening was done for, as far as any possibility of work was concerned. Even if she could go back upstairs in a quarter of an hour, her presence would remain. It wasn't like the middle ages any more, when you could simply drive out the evil spirits with incense.

His nerves revolted. Soon he would have to stick his fingers through the bars to show whether he was finally fat enough to be devoured. All the fears of his childhood descended on him, everything horrible that had oppressed him, that lay in wait for him behind every door, in ever newer and more frightful shapes, until they coalesced to the size of death on horseback. Now they were there again: the Persians who whipped him so that he would worship fire, the evil fairy with the spindle on which he was to prick himself and sleep away through all that was beautiful; the wolf who lived in the park and who had instructions from his mother to gobble him up if he loitered around on his way home from school, the snake in the attic that came gliding down the bell cord into his room, the murderer in the newspaper who cut the throats of a family of five in a nearby village and who, for certain, was lying under his bed right now, the snow in which he drowned, the horse that was going to bite him, the devil in the Punch and Judy show, and the devil's scolding grandmother from whom he'd run away screaming. But now he could no longer run away.

Finally the van Lier woman came back. It was as if Mama, after she'd let him cry a good, long time, was bending down over his bed at last. He immediately felt nestled in, protected by her powerful bosom and the soft creaking of her corset.

"They were upstairs, three men, rang and rapped on the door. Then they left."

"Uff," went Sabine. "But the bird had flown the coop. Bet that got them mad." (Voice like a tin horn.)

"You can go back up now," said the Mejuffrouw. "The coast is clear."

"Me? Back up? Tonight? Not on your life."

"They never come back. Everyone knows that."

"Everyone knows that, my dear Juffrouw van Lier. But do the secret police know it, too? Better safe than sorry. That's been my motto for a long time. The gentleman here has started it, now he has to finish it. May nothing worse ever happen to him than having to spend the night with good old Sabine."

"That's no good," said the van Lier woman firmly. "This is no hiding place. I can't allow it. Mijnheer is ill, very ill. Excitement could kill him."

"Why should he get excited if they don't come back?"

The van Lier woman, beaten by her own argument, tried desperately to get out of it: "He will get upset if he notices that a stranger is in his home."

"He won't even notice it. And don't try to tell me that ladies never visit here. I simply won't go up there. Not tonight, anyway. Are you heartless?"

The big heart under the heaving bosom softened.

"Oh, well, for heaven's sake. If you're so afraid."

"Afraid? Me? Not a bit. I'm just not stupid. To go running into the hands of the secret police after all this would be just too idiotic."

Resignedly, Miss van Lier fetched linens and made up a bed on the sofa. Andreas's plea to let him spend the night in the living room, she rejected.

"Since there's no way around it, you can do whatever you wish in here. You have rented the room. The rest of the apartment belongs to Mijnheer."

"Thank God," said Sabine after the housekeeper had left. "Such an unpleasant person. So frightfully Dutch. Now we can make ourselves comfortable."

She took off her hat and put her swollen, veined legs up on a hassock. The cigarette hung from her lips.

"I swore by my dear, departed parents never to talk to a German unless it was under duress. But since we can't very well refuse to talk to each other for the whole night, I'll tell myself it's under duress. Hocus-pokus, we can talk. And why not? It's really a funny situation. Don't y'think so too? If someone came in, he'd call it racial pollution right off. But no one's going to come in. You have to be an optimist. 'A good conversation's half of life,' my dear, departed grandfather said, and he was a clever man. I just love having a good talk. And how often do you think you get the chance to have one in this hick town? Besides, I'm interested to hear the opinions of the *autre côté* for once. You get to be entirely one sided. Every time I get down to brass tacks with someone, they just fold up and start bawling. I always say you can overdo the moaning and groaning, although our situation is anything but rosy, of course. But it won't get any better from wailing all the time, right? I'd rather go by what the poet said: 'Whatever does not kill me strengthens me.' It's probably from Goethe, right? No? Well, so it's one of Schiller's quotable quotes. Sounds sort of like the one about the strong man bearing his fate. Really awesome, our German poets. The Hollanders just can't measure up with their old Vondel. Just between the two of us, there's not much going on at all here with the arts. I suffer from that too, because y'must know I'm an artistic person through and through. Photography *is* art. Or do you have a different opinion? Well, I don't mean to tell you what to think. A 'specially beautiful art because it's snatched right from real life. The camera doesn't lie. Some of my dear colleagues go so far as to not retouch pores or wrinkles, but if y'ask me that's perverse. Nobody gets a kick out of seeing how he really looks. And art is actually there to bring beauty into our lives. Agree? Obviously I'm against Hitler, but he's definitely got a point with his concept of art. When he's right, he's right. I'd chuck that abstract junk out of the museums, too. A woman with two heads belongs in a freak show, not in a gallery supported by public funds. You're making a face like somebody stepped on your toes. You're a painter, maybe? No? Didn't think so. You don't look like a painter. More like a lawyer. Not that either? Wait, don't tell me, lemme guess. Teacher? No? Doctor? No? Journalist? Well there you are, it's written all over your face. In my profession you get to have an eye for people. You sort of look right into their hearts. Now, if I really wanted to unload! 'Course, you know the fairy tale about the guy who flies through the streets at night and looks into the lighted windows? Well, it's just like that with photographers. We can look into people and see their futures gliding by. I'm telling it straight—their futures. I know, now you want to say that's all romantic hogwash, but little Sabine is just a romantic, to the bitter end. Thank God. The poor, honest servant girl comes to me just the same as the big boss, and in front of my camera they're all just people, plain and simple. At home in Kassel, of course, it wasn't necessary to go making fancied up copies of cooks' faces, I could be choosy. I had the whole *haute volée* for customers. Yeh, back then! (Singing) 'When I was still Prince of Arcady…' Those were the days. Even though I didn't get anything handed to me on a silver platter then, either. Little Sabine doesn't come from a rich family and success doesn't come easy. But that's the way it is, right? *C'est la vie.* All the nobility came to me, but what I liked even better, to be honest, was that happy little gang from the theater. There were free tickets galore. Little Sabine is crazy about the theater, or, I actually should say: was, because the dream is over. Prost Mahlzeit. Jews forbidden. But that's no great loss here, because even with the best intent, you couldn't say that there's much going on in the theater in Holland. Not a country favored by the muses. At home in Kassel it was phenomenal. Our dear old State Theater was well known as a springboard for Berlin. What-all I didn't see! The classics and modern things, operas, and even operettas, too. I love them best of all, so charming and light. When I'm standing in my darkroom, I sing all those delightful melodies to myself and it makes the work so much easier. You just need a little pick-me-up. I can tell you it was no piece of cake, starting all over again—I didn't have a red cent, only my camera. But with her camera, little Sabine can work wonders. D'you wanna see some photos? You prob'ly thought I was schlepping my lunch around in my knapsack. Did ya really think so? There are pictures in there, my Leica, and film. In one of those camps where there are so many people they'll probably need a photographer. Mementos for later. And even if I can do most anything, I'd rather stick with the kind of work I've already done. What ya know is what ya know. Or maybe not. Please, take a look for yourself. This charming girl is the Countess of Limburg-Stirum and that gentleman there is Professor Levy of the Jewish Council. You don't know what the Jewish Council is? Well, excuse me, are ya blind? Or haven't you ever looked out your window at night when all that ruckus with the trolley cars is going on? That's where you'll see the boys from the Jewish Council with their armbands. But you're probably sleeping and having sweet dreams, that's the prerogative of youth. How shall I put it? The Jewish Council is just the Jewish Council and whoever belongs to it has a stamp on his identification papers that says he's exempted from the work brigades until further notice. As long, that is, as the Mofs have use for him. Because they can't really do everything by themselves, they always have just a few of their little men standing around to see that everything is done nice and orderly. The rest of it, the whole organization and all the rigamarole, they've shoved off onto the Jewish Council. Where'd I stop? Oh, yeah, the photos. That's our operetta tenor from Kassel, a heartbreaker *comme il faut*—actually a little fat already, but I've retouched that out. Don't you think these newlyweds are darling? Weddings are my specialty. Frankly, nothing can go wrong at all with them, the worst drip looks pretty with a veil. You can hardly imagine how many weddings I've been to. Just not to my own. But that's me fate and only God knows why. I've certainly had enough admirers, one for every finger y'might say, I only would've had to grab one. But little Sabine is probably too picky and the right one just didn't come along. Yes I realize I'm getting off the point, I still wanna show you the photos. Here's an engagement picture not quite as flattering as the one with the wreath and veil, but still darling. Two such pretty young people. Gone already, matter of fact. Right away, with the first load. Back then, people weren't being rounded up yet, just got a notice to report to the railroad station, and, believe it or not, a lot of them actually went. But when less and less of them showed up, the Mofs changed their procedure. This baby that you probably recognize from the showcase downstairs, was also deported, with his parents, of course. Families do stay together. And this woman, according to the rumors, has fled through Belgium and France to Switzerland with her whole family. Awful foolish to risk such a long way, always among foreigners, and they look Jewish, to boot. And if they're caught, what good has it done them? Get sent up on criminal charges, likely to a concentration camp. And that's probably a lot more unpleasant than a labor camp. Although, in my opinion, even there things are horribly exaggerated. I already told you we're always falling apart and bawling and shaking with fear. No wonder, sometimes ya think the Gestapo just arranged things to scare the daylights out of us. In February '41 they rounded up four hundred young men in the Jewish Quarter and the following June three hundred here in Zuid. And whatta ya think, in October death notices for all seven hundred came from Mauthausen. Yes, Mauthausen, you don't know where that is? Back then, we didn't know either. A concentration camp in Austria. And letters came, besides—printed on proper writing paper—that those taken into protective custody were not allowed to have visitors, but could receive letters twice a month and buy newspapers in the camp. Sounds entirely plausible. And then in the space of a few months, seven hundred young guys are supposed to have died. Naturally, nothing but sadism toward the poor relatives, because seven hundred healthy young boys, they don't just up and die like that. Don't you agree? The real prophets of doom are of the opinion they've been killed, but that's laughable, such things don't happen, that's impossible, we're not living in the middle ages anymore. And I know my former countrymen inside out, a rough hide but good to the core anyway. For sure, the guys from Mauthausen are in another camp where they're not allowed to write. When I have to go away, I know I'll meet up with a whole bunch of friends. Or d'ya think I shouldn't go in any case? Ya just never know. Maybe you'll catch typhus and kick off. That'd be too bad. But I'd still like to see Hitler sitting on a bench and two Jews walk by and the one says, 'Hey, I think that's Hitler sitting there.' And the other one says, 'A nebbish, that Hitler.' Good, huh? Too bad it's not mine. You really made me feel like doing the disappearing act tonight, though, quite honestly I never thought about it before. Maybe I should, really, maybe it's dumb to go along with them. I'd really like to hear your opinion about it. Prob'ly you know more about it than we do. No? Y'don't? Or ya just don't wanna say? Well, you really don't seem very talkative at all. But at least you could give me something to eat. I'm hungry as a bear. Don't have much? It's not really necessary. A little wurst and cheese? Let's have it! No cake? How sad. Sabine has a little sweet tooth and excitement is known to stir up the appetite. The woods at home were always full of waxed paper from sandwiches, phenomenal I'm telling ya, the pretty countess with the charming baron that heartbreaker, such dear people my clients who've already been taken away the sacred art a little retouch that's the whole secret couldn't ya write something about it in the paper perhaps a lot would change and love, that's really something else and little Sabine and little Sabine and little Sabine…"

And on and on, for hours, without letup—it roared in his head, he tried not to listen, but her penetrating voice forced its way into his ears again and again. Exhaustion and sadness fell from the ceiling in clumps.

"Time to hit the hay," she said finally, yawning loudly and rising out of the cloud of blue smoke. "Turn around or you'll go blind."

He put his head in his hands, heard her fussing around; there was the soft rustling of silk, the smell of eau de cologne.

"I'll turn toward the wall, you may undress."

But he kept sitting there without moving. After a while she said, "Such a funny thing, you could laugh yourself to death, little Sabine ends up spending the night with a German. And besides that, you'd be amazed if I told you how long it's been since I slept in the same room with a man."

A gurgling laugh. She rolled up in a ball and soon her loud, satisfied snoring could be heard.

He didn't move until the trolleys came. Then he walked to the window and stared down at the thing he felt a strange compulsion to look at night after night, an evil fascination that led him into darker and darker depths.

Chapter 7

Two nights later, he couldn't stand it at the window. Fought for breath. Sticking pains made him grab at his heart. He had only one desire: to be out in the street!

Without thinking, he shoved his passport and press card into his pocket—a sleepwalker who reacts properly during his unconscious march over the roofs.

It was so dark that he stumbled, caught himself, felt a pain in his ankle, and limped across the street toward the trolleys and into the beams of the blue flashlights. One of the men with the dogs walked over to him, gruffly demanded to know what he was doing there, inspected his papers, and saluted. The dog was wagging his tail all the while, a beautiful wolf with big, intelligent eyes, trained to charge at fleeing people. Andreas loved dogs, but wished he had a revolver to shoot the dog and himself.

Blue-faced, cadaverously pale creatures pushed and shoved. Eyes dark as on Roman sarcophaguses. In the coffins lay love, love great and small, that had died with the dead.

"You can't see a thing," whispered a woman's voice. "If it were only daylight." And a man's voice answered, "This is scandalous, in the middle of the night!"

Suddenly the beautiful face of Edith Rosenbusch, petrified by sorrow, appeared in front of him. He had to be dreaming, because he saw it now wherever he looked, twenty times, thirty times, shimmering out of the deep darkness. Framed by black hair parted down the middle, it floated through the night.

He turned away, limped back across the street, felt his way up the steps that led to the door of the building, and tried to insert the key

into the lock. Then he heard breathing beside him, was at first paralyzed by fear, but quickly realized that it must be a Jew who'd run
away. He took the person by the arm, managed to open the door after
considerable trouble, and pushed him into the house. Led him up the
stairs—though he was so agitated he could hardly walk—down the
dark hallway and into his room. After he had covered the window he
turned on the light.

The brightness dazzled him; and he was dazzled by the Arab boy's
face. Daniel was standing in the middle of the room, arms and hands
pressed flat against his body, his head tilted a little to the side as if it
were too heavy to hold upright. That was how people looked when
they'd been hanged; those who had it all behind them and were
swinging peacefully in the wind.

Andreas, still by no means sure he wasn't imagining it all again,
asked, "You wanted to come to me?"

Daniel nodded and tried to force a smile, which became a
grimace, the face of a person being tortured. Scream, go ahead
and scream! With terror in his soft, animal eyes, he told how
they'd been taken away in the night, how he'd gone as far as the
trolleys, determined to get on and stay with his parents as long as possible, but when his mother had gestured to him more and more
urgently to flee, he'd finally slipped away between two cars, unnoticed by the dogs. The address he knew by heart; the building was
familiar.

That was more or less what the boy said, not his exact words.
Daniel's words no longer existed; they had evaporated as completely
as if they'd never been spoken. And regardless of how much time and
trouble Andreas spent trying to bring back their sound, it was useless.
He searched for the lost melody, searched, more than anything else,
for the intonation of the one word that his friend used, questioningly, mockingly, yet with unmistakable tenderness, when he called
him by name from the easy chair: Andreas. But he couldn't even find

these three syllables again, neither their duration, nor their pitch, nor their timbre.

The boy sat down on the same chair Sabine Lisser had occupied two nights before, bent over, and lowered his head.

Andreas leaned against the window and looked at him, filled with the tormenting astonishment that he was glad. Misery's beneficiary, death's profiteer. Fearful love that does not ask how dearly it is bought. Did he love Daniel? Had he loved Daniel? Can you love that which you are yourself? Can you love something that you yourself are not? You need someone to answer for you, who will remain behind when you're gone, a son, a pupil. What's a man worth if he doesn't have a son? A beloved picture of oneself, younger, less distorted, purer. Daniel, of all the people who'd crossed his path, was the closest.

He made a helpless movement toward Daniel's hair, but let his hand drop before it reached its destination. Time crept by. Even as the trolleys were rolling away, the boy did not move. Rigidity, the rigidity of a corpse. Lot's wife has seen the destruction of Sodom and Gomorrah, the world of shadows, how did Orpheus manage to have enough strength to go on? Silence, nothing but the breathing of two people holding a death watch for two others who were still alive. From the trolley car to the train. The train will travel east. The East is nothingness.

Terrible hour of castration; unbloody, with insidious poison that paralyzes the powers of procreation. As yet Andreas does not know, knows it just as little as the victims of Hiroshima who would escape the bomb, that they who have gotten away with their lives are doomed.

What does one actually know? The East—that is nothingness, a pessimistic hypothesis. So far, nothing has been mentioned about gas chambers, mass executions, death camps, selections, crematoriums, knocked-out gold fillings, carefully sorted clothing and indifferently piled mounds of corpses; no mention of roll calls, death marches, stone quarries, medical experiments, injections of air into veins, letting people freeze, beating them to death to the sound of parade music.

Nor do you yet realize that someday, when you do know all of that, nothing will change and you'll go on walking in the same old rut and waiting submissively, if somewhat uneasily, for the next catastrophe. And that, in the meantime, you'll bemoan your fate if you don't get your daily bath (but most of the time you do). As yet, you don't have any idea how easily you can live with a past you haven't faced up to and even if you suspected it, you wouldn't believe it.

He went on standing there, bashful and clumsy in the face of terrible pain. Should he try to give comfort—but how does one do that? He could not help the fact that his thoughts wandered; it was simply impossible to go on thinking for hours: he's here, he's here, he's here. (Naturally he thought about Daniel's parents, too, tried to imagine them on their way into the terrifying unknown, but that didn't work. For him, Edith would be standing in the doorway, smiling at her son for all time, the doctor half slumped behind his desk, listening.) The tension caused physical desire; he calculated his chances with the woman with the violet eyes. He now knew that she was the daughter of the colonial official, was married to someone in the Hague, who, as the van Lier woman disapprovingly said, did business with the Mofs. She came every Saturday morning at ten on the dot, no longer so brightly dressed as during the summer, but still quite colorful in a chic fall suit with a flowered scarf and a hat wound with bright ribbons. Whenever he met her in the hallway—and he always met her, they both knew how to arrange that—he got a longing glance from eyes that looked even bluer beneath darkened lids (the color of the Mediterranean during a storm). She laughed easily, was good-natured, accommodating; her voice cooed with sensuality. It was charming the way her brown temples disappeared beneath the blond curls. Firm, luxuriant flesh, good for holding onto—salvation perhaps.

The boy moved. Lifted his head, stretched his back, stood up; did everything slowly, carefully, as if he wanted to make sure he still could. Shuffled around the room.

Suddenly he saw the torn painting, shuddered, and began, finally, to cry. Andreas put his arm around his shoulder, pressed him down onto the sofa, and held him in his arms the entire night.

Chapter 8

INTO the dunes with the Porsche, to the grave. No, not quite. The last five hundred meters you have to go on foot, through yellow sand on a path made of clinkers. With an escort of gulls waiting for scraps of bread. A bouquet of tulips in hand. To tell lies to the dead, you don't come empty-handed.

He was ashamed of himself and threw the flowers away. (Deceit toward the gulls who plunged greedily.)

From a high pole, the flag of the Netherlands waved at half mast; there was no calm here. On an iron cross *aere perennis*, were the names of the twenty-one hostages shot by the Germans on this spot. Miep Dekker first; she was the only woman.

A woman? No. A girl. His girl. His? In the hallway between his room and the door to the apartment he had shown her how to kiss. Nothing more. There was no place they could be together, not even the street, the field, the forest. A Dutch patriot doesn't go with a German, not even if he's a "good one." Kisses in no man's land, between the trenches, in the dark. Her briefcase, in which the loaded revolver was concealed next to the English grammar book and her forged papers, bumped against his back during their embrace.

"Would you shoot?' he asked sarcastically, convinced that a schoolgirl doesn't shoot under any circumstances. She didn't understand the jibe. Sarcasm lay outside the range of her thinking. She thought like daughters of lesser civil servants the world over, in a straight line, sentimentally, with a dash of provincial newspaper and a dash of Hollywood, mixed, in her case with Calvinism.

"Of course," she said dryly.

Nothing happened in this tormented city that she didn't hear about in very little time. She came every day, on the run, and was the only tie to reality for him and Daniel.

Standing in front of the easy chair, turned more toward Daniel than toward him, she reported the arrests, executions, and deportations. At such moments, she excluded him. She said, "The Germans have…" not "The Nazis…" He belonged with the Germans and nothing could be done about it.

One day she told about Daniel's cousin, Susanne Rosenbusch, who'd given away the address of her hiding place when arrested on the street. "They found a list of names of resistance people there. Twenty-four of them were picked up. Of course she only did it out of stupidity. But she ought to be bumped off anyway." Without pity, like a judge of the Nazi "People's Court."

Didn't she know that Susanne and Daniel were related? His narrowed eyes, his pressed lips should have given her a sign. But she said once more, "Yes, bump her off." She made no allowance for feelings toward relatives and would have delivered her own sister to the knife. Everything was either black or white—death for the evil ones, life for the righteous. "Righteous" was anyone who stuck by Holland. That simple.

Miep didn't know any other country than this one; for her it was the world. The world had to be free again. And then everything would be all right. "How do you envision freedom, Miep?" An astonished look from the somewhat too bright eyes. Was he making fun of her? "Freedom is when the Dutch can decide what goes on in their country again." "Doesn't matter in what form?" "Doesn't matter." She made no great demands. Politics interested her only in connection with the resistance.

What really did interest her? What would you have been able to talk about with her in normal times? Probably nothing. She didn't think much of art. That was useless junk, time frittered away. She never expressed the wish to read anything by him. (For which he was grateful.) Writing she viewed as a remunerative activity, like sitting-behind-a-counter-and-selling-stamps. She was brought up to cook a man his meals and darn his socks. For that, he would take her to the movies and sleep with her.

Disconsolate life, practiced for generations and passed on, over and over again. In this gray, scullery maid's existence, hopeless from the very beginning, appeared the unexpected beacon of the resistance. The call to life. The calling. The battle-cry resounds and the trumpets blare. Even if, as is proper in this country, somewhat mutedly. You are not a visionary, Catholic peasant girl who hears voices, but a sober young miss, a meisje who does not aspire to lead the troops and bring the queen back to the Hague; you do what you think is necessary and human, without a fuss, with self-evident modesty. But, still, deeply convinced of the grace that has been bestowed on you by the fact that you may do it.

She came running in, blond, thin, on lanky legs; gave her aunt, the van Lier woman, a kiss; gave her report, conversed a short time with Daniel—in the language of seventeen-year-olds which Andreas didn't understand even then, when he could already speak Dutch quite well—and then had to be on her way: someone in hiding needed forged ration cards, a Jewish child smuggled out of a deportation column was to be turned over to foster parents, contact needed to be established between a Dutch officer and a boatman who could take him to England. An embrace in the dark hallway. Unsatisfying, frayed the nerves. When she was gone, her carefree child's laughter remained behind. And only the rolling of the trolleys made it die away.

But on a Monday night in the fall the trolleys didn't come. He was standing at the window; Daniel was asleep. It was two o'clock. He listened. It got to be half-past two and still there was nothing. He should have been happy, but he was afraid. Terror had become a habit; any change threatened the laboriously constructed basis of existence. The rolling of the trolley cars was the theme from which the fugue of the night developed. What was to become of it in the soundless darkness?

He leaned way out. The wind was blowing, searchlights were probing the sky. There was still a war on.

The failure of the trolleys to show up seemed all the more incomprehensible to him. Had the order to stop come from some higher command? Whoever was responsible for all of it could be dead, or might have fallen into disfavor. Perhaps they were out of railroad cars, or coal; perhaps the camps were filled to the bursting point (he caught himself again and again avoiding the thought of murder). Nothing was impossible, everything could go back to what it was before. Everything, but not him. The rolling of those trolley cars had disassembled him into his components, into seeing eyes, hearing ears, a beating heart, twitching nerves, and blood that was running out drop by drop. How was he ever going to put all that together again? He wasn't a god. He'd never again make a poet out of the pieces in this life.

For him it was all over, not for the others. The Rosenbusches would come home, Edith even paler, the doctor with even rounder shoulders. And Daniel would get up from his easy chair (now he did so rarely and unwillingly—what was the point, when walking around was only a fiction?) and finally have to answer the question that had been asked of him over and over again—what was he thinking of doing after the war—to which he now reacted only with a resigned shrug of his shoulders, with pain in his eyes that was both new and as old as the millenium. A seventeen-year-old who denied any "afterward" was the most horrible contradiction; only very old people were allowed to live their lives one day at a time. But perhaps a Jew could only ever give an answer based on the past, that heavy weight he drags around with him, that takes the lightness from his stride, the gracefulness from his bearing, the candor from his speech, and that makes him suspicious in the eyes of others and humiliates him in his own. A Jew who believes in the future is deceiving himself.

And so Daniel would get up and return to his parents, and the present, the horrible, splendid present, would come to an end. With all that future, there wouldn't be any present anymore; writing is future, the word that has taken shape is already groping for the next one. I am becoming, but I no longer am.

Being shut in this room with Daniel was the present. Without a past, without a future. The ugly furniture, the South Sea bric-a-brac, the blackout paper on the window, the torn painting, the van Lier woman's huge bosom, Miep's laughter, the footsteps of the doctor who came to see the colonial official daily, the langorous looks of the violet-eyed woman, the groping fingers of the searchlights, the barking of the flak, the black of night, the trolley cars—present, everything present. The moment that lingers on. The unshakeable illusion of immortality.

When Daniel came to stay with him, he stopped writing. (It wasn't only the boy: now even *he* refused to questions about the future.) Sebastian L. had died quickly and painlessly, and no tears were shed over him. But he left Daniel under the impression that his not writing was a sacrifice made for him. Following the principle: If I'm not alone, I can't work. The only lie between them. Embellished with senseless flourishes like "creative pause," and so on.

They turned out the newspaper articles together. Daniel's favorite occupation: thumbing his nose at the enemy. It all sounded quite plausible, was witty and amusing (promptly resulting in praise from the newspaper for the so much more relaxed style), gave the impression of being conformist, but, between the lines, there were sparks. Daniel sat in the easy chair, dictating; he typed at the little round table.

When they were finished, they engaged in an ongoing conversation that never lost its intensity. He'd always been left to his own devices; now a voice provided answers, demanded its turn to be heard. The dialogue had moved out of the sphere of chance encounter and had become the real form of life. Often, they talked on past the hour of the trolley cars, far into the morning. He was ahead of the boy in many respects, in his knowledge of literature and philosophy, experience with women, travel, interpretation of dreams, and power of expression. Against that, Daniel possessed a more attentive relationship to reality. His life had been, despite emigration and persecution, happy; that may have been the reason for his lack of inhibitions. Andreas discovered that between parents and children there could be a matter-of-fact feeling of belonging together, tolerance, and encouragement of talent, where, in his own home, there had been nothing but opposition, misunderstanding, the struggle of the weak against the strong. Sometimes he thought it had been made too easy for Daniel to just play with his talents: he painted, wrote, was interested in pedagogy, sociology, history, knew a lot about his father's profession, loved the theater, developed ideas about directing, had experimented with a 35mm camera, and on top of that, was a good swimmer, skier, and tennis player. But he seemed to have done all that as a sideline to the main duty of being his parents' child. He still held on tightly to this role; here his sense of reality had failed him. He refused to grow up. That became most noticeable in his dealings with the housekeeper, who loved him fanatically from the start; there was never any talk of *his* not being able to stay, the sick Mijnheer no longer seemed to be important. Daniel was her child and she his mother. He let himself be spoiled by her, called her his *Nonitschka* and put up with her displays of tenderness with astonishing patience.

With the same passion with which he carried on a conversation, Daniel read. Shakespeare, Goethe, Thomas Mann, murder mysteries, Dostoyevsky, Rilke, Proust, Homer, Marx, Hegel, Nietzsche, and newspapers—the little Resistance four-pagers that Miep brought and the big German ones, with their half-truths and bombastic speeches. He read without getting tired, like one who knows he doesn't have much time, one who wants to learn something about the world and life and has no means other than the printed word. Hunger for love, adventure, foreign countries, big cities, the sea and meadows, nightclubs, movies, theaters, concerts; for other sounds, other smells, other colors; a hunger for experience, a glutton shaking with greed, who cries out for new and different foods at every meal but stuffs himself full of pap.

Andreas's hands were clenched around the iron cross. Tears ran down his face. He hadn't cried since the end of the war. It didn't bring any relief. Nothing brought any relief. Those mild ghosts, his uncle and aunt, had long since been pushed aside by the demon that was making him rot away even while conscious and alert.

There was no longer any refuge in illusion, as there had been at that time of happiness outside the "law" when he believed that the narrow island he was living on with Daniel was safe from the racing current of the war.

He cried more despairingly.

No, said Susanne, with unmoved eyes.

Then he stopped crying.

Read the names of the patriots and those who just happened along by chance—it was known that a recently apprehended black-marketeer and an old gent who'd forgotten his indentity papers had been included. Executed, because an SS leader had come away from an assassination attempt with a flesh wound of the arm.

He looked for Daniel's name, although he knew it wasn't there. The irrational hope of finding it anyway. For the Jews who put up resistance, there was no merciful, quick death. A Jew belongs in a concentration camp.

He didn't go on thinking. For years, his self-preservation mechanism reacted when his thoughts approached Daniel in the concentration camp.

Instead of that he asked himself: what would have become of Daniel?

A question without an answer. Daniel was seventeen, would always remain seventeen. Without the murdering hands of his torturers, he would have fallen prey to the torture of becoming a man. No way out. He cried again. The wind blew. Above him the gulls were screaming.

Chapter 9

THE trolleys no longer came, but the deportations went on. They'd managed to think up something new, were taking the Jews to a collection center, an old, come-down theater (repertoire: popular plays and farces), and sending them in police vans—when they'd rounded up enough—to a railroad loading ramp far from the city.

On Beethovenstraat, the nights were quiet. Now and then a car drove by, sometimes you heard footsteps and listened. If it was the tread of jackboots, you stayed put, motionless, rigid with fear. Often there were air raid sirens, the antiaircraft guns fired, the planes that were flying to Germany droned by at high altitude. Then the sirens again, and silence. It was the silence, more than anything that chased away sleep. It settled deceptively over the world and swallowed up murder, manslaughter, shrieks of pain, and the raging of battles.

He waited for whatever would come. Time had broken in on him and he was again condemned to bearing witness. Miep had to tell him, him directly; he wormed it out of her, and her "…the Germans have…" no longer affected him. He wanted to know everything: what, where, when, how many dead, how many arrested, how many sent away. But even that wasn't enough, he had to see for himself, struck out on his own, walked through the Euterpestraat, where Gestapo Headquarters and the "Central Authority for Jewish Emigration" were housed in two schools that stood directly opposite each other. (Emigration, that is, deportation; Work Brigade, that is, concentration camp; the East, that is, nothingness.) Two schools with big glass windows, colored mosaics, modern and solid buildings—nothing more was to be seen. In front of the Dutch Schouwburg Theater, the collecting point in the Jewish quarter, an SS man was standing guard. His cap at an angle, he was leaning against the wall watching the girls; then he lit up a cigarette, crossed one leg over the other, and whistled a hit song. No, he wasn't standing guard, he'd just come out of the building to catch a little air, was hiding from work and behaving just like any good-looking twenty year-old. That had nothing to do with war and destruction. It was hard to be a witness where nothing was happening.

Once, in the city, a truck with prisoners drove by—they were workers, sitting on benches, hands in their laps. Watched by two soldiers with rifles at the ready. Why didn't they resist, forty against two, beat up their guards, run away? What kind of magic power does a rifle have over people?

Had he imagined that something could be made of this kind of testimony in the future? That he was the only one who could write and who knew what was going on? There were reports by people who'd been in the concentration camps, who'd been tortured and condemned to death, diaries of concentration camp commandants, of people who'd gone into hiding, resistance fighters, officers, material that hadn't been organized and some that had been, reams of reports, last letters, eyewitness accounts, court testimonies taken down by a stenotypist or recorded on tape, novels, short stories, poems, radio dramas, stage plays, films. In the beginning, nobody wanted to see, hear, or read them; war again already, persecution again, nightly air raids again, all so long ago; and only when it had gotten to be even longer ago did people get used to accepting it, a little astonished, a little revolted, yes, that's the way it was, horrible, as in Roman times, as in the Middle Ages, the world never changes, how cruel the French were to the Algerians, how bad the blacks have it in America. Experienced, educated, culture-pessimistic, they arranged everything they learned in their card-files, for science, for posterity, for doctoral theses in the year 3000. Physicians faced by the phenomenon of cancer that they were fighting as best they could; not lovers, who, with a scream, threw themselves on the decomposed bodies of their beloved. They accepted it, there was nothing they were not prepared to accept, even fear of the bomb, even the knowledge that people could be manipulated. They could live with all that and be happy, the ones who were fit, all of them. But he was groping around in the dark, and whatever he grabbed hold of was made of fluff, without contour.

He had the notebook from those days on the undersized hotel-room table in front of him and was reading:

In Rotterdam, police round up young Dutchmen who are sent to Germany as workers. 540 caught.

In the Hague, 22 Bible scholars arrested. Sent to Buchenwald.

In retribution for the murder of a member of the secret police, a villa in the Apollolaan burned down. The inhabitants have ten minutes to leave the building.

Professor S., a Jew, previously chairman of mathematics, takes poison as he is about to be taken away. His wife is dragged away from the dying man.

K. A., a girlfriend of Miep's, attempts to flee on her bicycle, along with her brother, after they are caught by the secret police distributing illegal newspapers. A shot smashes both her kneecaps. Her brother manages to get away. The girl lies in the street for six hours before anyone is allowed to help her.

Obersturmbahnführer A.d.F. takes his Dutch girlfriend with him to the Schouwburg to see the interned Jews.

Sick Jews are being rounded up according to special lists. Today four dead, even before they reach the train. The corpses are transported with the others.

L. M., a laborer, had hidden two Jewish children in his home. Arrested a month age, taken away, destination unknown. Now his wife gets a death notice from Sachsenhausen.

Frau D., a colleague of Sabine Lisser's who works for the Jewish

Council in the Schouwburg, comes and asks whether we can find her a copy of *War and Peace.* For the first time (and she'd been working there for months) a detained Jew (a nineteen-year-old) has expressed the wish for a book. (She tells about the kinds of things the arrested people want—mostly from their own homes—among other things, tea services, canaries, expensive fur coats, and toasters.) I find *War and Peace;* when Frau D. goes to the Schouwburg next morning, the boy has already been called up for transport.

All the inmates of the Jewish Mental Clinic at Apeldoorn Bosch are sent away. Since there is insufficient room in the freightcars, the 1300 patients (among them several healthy people who thought an insane asylum would be a safe hiding place) are piled on top of each other.

During his interrogation, the Communist physician Dr. G. uses his bound hands to knock down a Gestapo man and throws himself out of a fifth-floor window. Killed instantly.

The Jewish photographer B. has posed as a Gestapo agent for a year and delivered important information to the underground movement. Is betrayed. While being arrested he kills two secret policemen, then shoots himself.

Two hundred Jewish orphans deported.

Miep brings a call-up order for the work brigades (someone from the Jewish Council has smuggled it out of the Schouwburg). The Dutch security agent who had delivered one Jew as ordered had noted on it: "Ran down two more on my own." Underneath a receipt for nine Guldens. So they're getting three Guldens for each Jew.

All things that he knew only from hearsay; but he had seen the burned-out house.

He leafed through the notebook. Finally he found something that he himself had overheard.

At D. G.'s.

Daisy Goedhart, the violet-eyed woman. His first visit to her house. Invitation for cocktails, Tuesday at half past five. From her glances, he assumed he'd be alone with her. But when a maid in a black dress, white apron, and lace cap opened the door ("Finally you're getting to meet some decent people," Mama would have said), he heard sounds from within, screeching laughter. He wanted to leave right away, but Daisy came running out and dragged him into the room, screaming loudly. He was her catch; she was proudly putting him on display.

The room, in turn-of-the-century style, dark, overloaded, a heavy Dutch chest with Delft china behind glass, landscapes and still lifes on the walls; huge, immovable furniture, richly carved, on oriental rugs. Floor lamps with brocade shades, and hanging from the ceiling, a chandelier of Venetian glass.

Daisy had let go of him. He was standing around alone, smoke stinging his eyes. A blond, heavily made-up person pressed a glass of champagne into his hand and said drunkenly, "Prost."

A mixture of German and Dutch was being spoken, a German officer was fondling a girl, all the rest were civilians, some fifteen or twenty of them, a tall red-faced man shook his hand so hard it hurt, and said he was happy to meet him. Probably the master of the house, no introduction offered.

When no one else paid any attention to him, he sat down on a sofa beside a man who mumbled his name so badly that he didn't understand it, so he called him "Herr X" in the notes he made the following morning.

Herr X was stocky, jovial, the kind of good-humored uncle who carries bags of candy in his pockets for his dear nephews and nieces. Herr X had no face, although of course you could pick out eyes, nose, and mouth; but no matter how often you looked at him, they seemed to be shoved under one another, stretched out, or pushed together. Herr X owned, as he related at length, a chemical factory in Wuppertal. But first and foremost, Herr X was a stamp collector and made pronouncements like: "Collecting is, in general, uncommonly educational. It demands concentration and forms character. Collecting stamps, in particular, opens up the world. It awakens interest in other countries, educates and exercises the eye, and elevates one's understanding of art. Collectors are patient people."

A gray-haired, shabbily clothed Dutchman joined him, sat down on one of the oversized chairs, but just on the edge, as if he wanted to jump up again at any moment. In his left hand he held a glass, and in his right a bottle of champagne from which he filled his glass over and over again. He looked like a tax collector (Just the very way you'd imagine a tax collector—a lower-level civil servant with a penchant for chopping off heads), but was, as it soon turned out, a stamp dealer.

With heads close together, but uninhibited by his presence, the two men held a conversation that he wrote down the next morning:

Dealer: Would you be interested in the collection of Samuel Guggenheim?

Herr X: Would I? You're quite a joker. That's one of the best collections around. Something the likes of us can only dream about. Old Guggenheim was perhaps the greatest expert we had. Has he emigrated to Holland? Someone told me America. Well—that's his business. America would probably have been better for him. He doesn't really want to sell?

Dealer: I don't think Guggenheim *wants* to sell.

Herr X: Well, so what's all the talk about?

Dealer: It's not just talk. Or do you think I'm putting you on? Very likely I can get the collection for you. Are you interested?

Herr X: Of course! What a question. I can't think of anything I'd rather have. But the whole thing sounds a little funny. Guggenheim doesn't want to sell but he's selling anyway. What's that supposed to mean? I always prefer to have things done nice and clean. Is Guggenheim in some sort of trouble?

Dealer: How am I supposed to answer that? A Jew—these days!

Herr X: Well, of course. I just heard yesterday that they're also taking measures against the Jews here in Holland. But still, like I always say, Jews are human, too.

Dealer: Whatever. But let's leave Guggenheim out of the deal. Guggenheim doesn't have anything more to say about it. He won't even find out what happens to his collection. And I don't think he'd care, anyway.

Herr X (*in a tone of genuine regret*): Oh. I understand. They've taken him away already.

Dealer: Not yet. The second Guggenheim's gone, the collection's out of our reach. There are a lot of people just waiting for it. But don't worry. We'll land this one yet. We just have to reel it in bit by bit.

Herr X: I don't understand.

Dealer: Move by move. First one, then the next.

Herr X: Which one? Which next?

Dealer: First we say we want the collection. Then Guggenheim and his family are taken away.

Herr X: Who's we? You and I? Or are there other people involved?

Dealer: Naturally. I can't do this alone. But you only have to deal with me.

Herr X: Is he going to be taken away for sure?

Dealer: Who? Guggenheim? As certain—how do you say it in German—as Amen in church.

Herr X: And how are you going to find out about the time?

Dealer: I don't find out about it, I determine it. And since you're right here, it'd be best if we took care of things immediately. Tonight.

Herr X: No, no, no! I'm not getting involved in that. No way.

Dealer: It doesn't matter a bit whether he has to leave a few weeks earlier or later.

Herr X: No, no.

Dealer: Perhaps it's really just a few more days. There aren't many more Jews in Holland. Quite possibly he'd be going away today or tomorrow even without our being involved.

Herr X: Then we can just wait too.

Dealer: How often do I have to tell you that I won't even be able to get near the collection then? We have to get the ball rolling.

Herr X: Not me! I'm not going to do such a thing.

Dealer: Do you want the collection? Yes or no?

Herr X: Naturally I want it. But not *that* way.

Dealer: It's no good any other way. May I mention, in addition, that you'll get the collection unusually cheaply. I'd judge for about half the actual value.

Herr X: Oh God, oh God! But I can't. Impossible.

Dealer: It's not a matter of what you can do, I'll take care of everything myself.

Herr X: Why have you gone and told me all this? Why didn't you simply come and say, "Here's the Guggenheim collection"?

Dealer: You're a good one! My dear sir, there's a war on, most people have no desire to buy, nine-tenths of my customers were Jews. Unfortunately, I don't have enough capital at my disposal to take over the collection. What would happen if I were stuck with it?

Herr X: But you won't be. I want it anyway.

Dealer: Well, there we are, that sounds better already.

Herr X: You really think he could be leaving tomorrow anyway?

Dealer: Or the day after tomorrow, or at the latest in a few weeks. It makes no big difference to Guggenheim. But to us...

Herr X: Does anyone actually know where the Jews are going?

Dealer: To Germany, for the work brigades. Doesn't hurt them a bit to learn for once what work means.

Herr X: Guggenheim is an old man. And even ten years ago had a severe heart condition.

Dealer: Then he's hardly likely to have to work. There are homes for the elderly, after all.

Herr X: Homes for the elderly, too? That's reassuring. You know, we hear so little about these things in Germany. Well, for heaven's sake then, OK.

Dealer: Now you just have to tell me how high I can go. (*They put their heads together and whisper.*)

They had to be drunk—everyone in that room was—otherwise, they'd hardly have spoken so loudly that he could hear them; only when it came down to figures did the merchant's customary circumspection begin to function.

Cold sweat stood out on his forehead when he heard the dealer telephoning in the adjoining room. (He could understand, "Jawohl, Herr Obersturmbahnführer.") Herr X stared at his pudgy hands and said mournfully, "One feels as if one were stealing from a corpse."

Andreas leaned forward: "It's not a matter of stealing from corpses here, it's a matter of…"

A cloud of perfume closed off his mouth. He mumbled the word "murder" into a warm hand. "Idiot," whispered Daisy, "think of Daniel."

She was smarter than he was, more cunning. He obediently fell silent, admired her, and only then did it occur to him: How does she know about Daniel? Miep, the van Lier woman, they're the only ones in on it, it was unthinkable that they'd talked. Can't you trust anyone anymore?

He drank. Champagne at first, then wine, then cognac. Someone was always pushing something to drink at him, he wan't used to it, slowly he began to drift off, the room dissolved. Herr X became blurred, then the dealer, two giant paws lifted their glasses and toasted each other. Andreas grabbed at his: "Long live Guggenheim!" They laughed and returned his toast: "Long live Guggenheim!" Daisy came—brightly colored fabric and perfume and blond hair—sat down beside him on the arm of the sofa and put her hand on his shoulder. He pressed his head against her firm hip, lay as if in a warm bath, relaxed. The room began to revolve slowly, but it wasn't unpleasant, actually more amusing, a very gentle, rocking carousel.

When he did get a little bit dizzy anyway, he closed his eyes, until she bent down toward him so far that her hair tickled his ear. "Come. You need some sleep."

He got up. She led him; without help he would have sat down again immediately. The trip to the second floor seemed like climbing a mountain. The room into which she took him was dimly lighted, there was only a red-shaded lamp burning in front of a mirror. She helped him off with his jacket, he pushed his shoes off himself, then fell into bed; it was soft, smelled of Daisy's perfume. His head was lying on lace and silk.

"What do you know about Daniel?"

"Later." She kissed him on the forehead, with maternal tenderness: the sick child who does not have to go to school, who can lie in mother's bed and close his eyes in broad daylight.

Falling asleep, he heard the familiar sounds of his sore-throat-and-upset-stomach days: the blinds being let down, someone coming and going, a book being put away, a glass being pushed back, and as something new, a fresh, swirling cloud of perfume.

Then he awakened for the first time in that bedroom, in that passionate movie-goer's dreamworld, decorated with ribbons, bows, and puffy lace curtains; blinked at the billowing purple of the canopy, and saw, turning his head, a lilac-colored monkey sending him a melancholy look from the night table. The perfume was strong and close by. Daisy said, "Nobody else is home. Even my husband has gone out." Then she lay down beside him.

When evening and the vulgar grotesqueness of the room had returned, he asked while he was getting up, "What do you know about Daniel?"

Had he really believed she wouldn't notice that another person was living in his room? She'd returned at an unaccustomed time, "on Miss van Lier's afternoon off, while you were out, too," and had gone in. "Was he frightened?" "Just a little," she said and laughed tenderly. The tenderness disconcerted him. "Do you like him?" "He's a beautiful boy."

That was all. He learned nothing more, neither that evening nor later.

At first it bothered him, but after a while, he reconciled himself to it and began to imagine that there had been something between those two whom he loved in such different ways. In reality, he didn't believe so at all, although there were several things in favor of it: Daisy's tender voice and Daniel's silence about her visit; Daisy's eyes, swollen from crying, after Daniel was gone. His beauty and her sensuality.

He was jealous and enjoyed his jealousy. Jealous of a dead man and of someone who was even further beyond reach than if she had been dead—an aging, middle-class matron, probably long since widowed (her husband was thirty years older than she), now totally addicted to a vice she'd previously practiced: eating cake.

He pulled the two pictures from his wallet. One of Daniel, postcard-sized. Sabine Lisser had taken it; in the lower right-hand corner was her name, ornate and stupid (an artist signs things). It was a bit too slick, too dramatically lighted, too heavily retouched. Daniel looked like a movie actor in the role of Daniel. More delicate than in reality, without the irony that was part of him, exaggeratedly melancholic.

On a 2¼" x 3¼" snapshot, a slightly blurred Daisy in a flowered bathing suit was sitting on the beach, laughing. In the background, a gray expanse of waves, the ocean. Nothing about her was recognizable except that she was blond and chubby.

He had nothing more of them than two photos. Blurred and retouched. He was even a poor witness for his love.

Chapter 10

THE train, unheated and dark, was traveling through the night from the Hague to Amsterdam. It was snowing. From time to time, searchlights probed the sky. People were talking all around him. He was gradually beginning to understand the language. The conversations all revolved around the same thing: where can one still get food? They didn't risk talking about other things on a train. But without their having said anything, hatred of the Germans came through.

Wearily, he pressed his head against the smooth wood. Exhausted from lovemaking. Hung over. With a guilty conscience for having left Daniel alone so long. Impatient because the train was going so slowly and delaying his return home.

He pictured this homecoming in his imagination. The room is warm, Daniel is sleeping; he doesn't turn on the light so as not to waken him; he undresses quickly and goes to bed. He could never imagine sleeping in the same room with another person. Now it's perfectly natural. His own home. With Daniel and the headless birds and the South Sea bric-a-brac. Even the two masks are hanging on the wall again—Daniel thinks they're hilarious. The lace doily on the table. The brass bed. The green sofa with the torn, spotted, covering. Daniel's easy chair, upholstered in dark red with carved lion heads at the ends of the arm rests. It all fits together, it's just right. His room in Munich could be found in any interior-decorating magazine. The son's room, the room of a young poet: the big desk, gleaming and tidied up, the baroque commode, the many well-arranged books, everything within easy reach, the wide, dark gray couch, two drafts-man's lamps that can be bent in all directions, the picture of Positano that Hans painted when they were there together, the piece of a Greek vase he found in Segesta. The always-fresh flowers that Mama put there. Spotless, not a speck of dust. View of the garden. How beautiful, say the visitors: this is the life. They're wrong. To be sure, it's not a place for nightmares, and probably that's what they mean with their praise, since they're all so busy escaping nightmares. And certainly not one where a girl's laughter remains suspended in the air.

Softly, on tiptoe, he entered the apartment, carefully depressed the handle of the door to his room. A light was on. Daniel was standing at the window, sullen and tired from lack of sleep; in Daniel's easy chair, smoking, legs crossed, the veiled hat on her head, sat Sabine Lisser.

"Better late than never," she called out. "And he doesn't even know he's missed a real, genuine *razzia*. But this time I was brave as can be and came downstairs all by my lonesome. Was absolutely necessary, they broke in the door to my apartment and poked through everything. Not even Juffrouw van Lier thinks I can go back up there again. And with that the die would seem to have been cast. Here I am and here I stay."

There she was and there she stayed. She spread all over the apartment. Sprayed her poison. Shattered their nerves, talking from morning till night.

Miep found her a new hiding place, but she refused to go there. Said she didn't feel safe among strangers. Would the others feel responsible if something happened to her? The others wouldn't. People in hiding were sacrosanct. Which didn't exclude their occasionally being used as cheap—or even more often, paying—household servants by people who would have loved to be antisemitic but couldn't be, simply because it was the fashion for Dutch nationalists to be of the opposite opinion from their hated enemies about everything. To deliver Sabine into the hands of such people was impossible. Maybe the van Lier woman or Miep would have done it despite everything; he, however, was hindered by his German guilt complex.

Daniel hated Sabine, was sick with hate. But he too had to put up with her. Damned solidarity. They should have sent her away. To the other people. Or simply out into the street. What do we care about this woman?

Her voice (tin horn, file against glass) the whole day. First thing in the morning, she'd shuffle through the apartment in bathrobe and slippers. "Good morning, you dear people." Always the same beginning. The first splashes of the torrent to follow. Sabine's dreams, Sabine's insomnia, Sabine's grand nighttime adventures, Sabine's hunger, Sabine's gratification, Sabine's joy over the beautiful weather and Sabine's annoyance about the bad weather, Sabine's hatred of the Nazis, Sabine's aversion toward Holland, Sabine's opinions and thoughts about the war, the baker's helper, the illness of the colonial official, Miep's brazenness, old Dutchmen, the underground's Radio Oranje, Sabine's memories of Kassel, Sabine's successes, Sabine's art. It didn't stop until late at night when, once more, she stuck in a head covered with curlers: "Good night, you dear people. Sleep well, sweet dreams." Andreas could get away, but Daniel was mercilessly exposed to her.

Daniel's brightness faded. The newspaper articles became dull and humorless. He got up from his armchair even less than before. Blinked, with animal eyes that had become lackluster, at the sun that showed through the window in the mornings. Eyes like those of a dog that's begging to go along, out into the street. Each time it was necessary to say no. No, no, no.

Miep was the only one who didn't have to say no. She told about the resistance, soberly, without embellishment, and probably without even being aware, herself, how enticing and seductive it was that way. About waiting in the meadows at night until the plane came from London with the forged identity papers and took back a Dutch passenger; about crawling up banks to the bridges where they tied the explosives; about attacking registration offices in order to burn all the records; about girls disguised as cleaning women who spied on German installations, about boys trained as snipers, ready to attempt an assassination. Wild West stories, full of the romance of childhood; anyone hearing about them would have no doubt that dilettantes were playing war here and risking human lives. Least of all Daniel, the sceptic, who'd resolved to try to save himself, to hold out in his easy chair, to resist going along to the slaughter that had been ordained for the likes of him. So far, his eyes were not begging Miep to take him along; when she was there, they looked serious and severe. He fought with himself, was disciplined, and didn't ask for a thing. But it was still easy to see that he was becoming more restless from day to day and expressing less and less criticism of Miep's stories.

It was not just the Lisser woman that drove him from safety, even if, without her, he might have been able to keep himself under control longer. His nerves just couldn't take it longer, the voluntary banishment to the easy chair became torture—and the realization that his contemporaries were fighting against Germany all over the world. He didn't say it, these days he hardly said anything. The running conversation was broken off; they were often silent even at night when they were alone.

Andreas quarreled with the boy, thought he was undisciplined and a grumbler. Basically, Daniel had it good, far better than most of those who'd gone into hiding. Naturally Sabine was a pain, but everyone had to make some sacrifice these days. Even *he* had to put his work aside in order to rescue Daniel. (Did he really believe that?)

More and more often, he went to visit his loyal mistress Daisy, that little tart whose partial understanding didn't allow her to grasp the whole situation, the tragic aspects of war and occupation ("Am I helping anyone by being sad?"), but who functioned astonishingly well in everyday matters. Traitor, the Dutch would call her one day, collaborator, German whore—possibly they'd even shave off her hair and lock her up because she was nice to the German officers who brought her Chanel from Paris. Without this perfume (much too much of it), she claimed, she couldn't exist; probably she'd read that it was all the rage among the fashionable set in Paris and to be a *grande dame* was her most fervent wish. She wasn't one and never would be. Great ladies have bearing and character. She didn't have that, but on the other hand, she was willing to do anything for a friend. And however little feeling she might have had for what was in good taste, she had a great deal for what was the right thing to do at the right moment.

She wasn't in agreement with the fact that the Lisser woman was also living in her father's apartment now, but was much too good-natured to throw her out. And so Sabine stayed on, went on sleeping in the van Lier woman's room, which had been magnanimously vacated for her, but which she called a despicable hole nevertheless, thereby letting it be known she would not stay there during the day and that there was simply nothing other for her to do than sit in Andreas's room. ("Although you get on my nerves horribly, my dears. This boor won't even get out of his comfortable chair to make room for a lady.") The housekeeper had set up her bed in the living room, which was separated from the colonial official's bedroom only by a sliding door. Mijnheer was told that this way she was better able to look after him during the night. He needed the looking after, poor, terminally ill man; he was becoming weaker and weaker, more and more disoriented (as Daisy reported with moist eyes now, whenever she came from her father), so that it could be assumed he wouldn't grasp what was going on in his nice, middle class apartment, with those Indonesian souvenirs that gave it such a disagreeably exotic touch.

A few times he did ask anyway, startled out of a shallow sleep by his racking cough, what the voices and footsteps in the hall could possibly mean; but the van Lier woman knew how to quiet him down by saying with a sigh—which she repeated loudly and with unexpected comic talent when she recounted the story—that the gentleman lodger whom they'd been forced to take in by the Germans was once again having visitors.

One morning, after she'd entered his room exactly at eight as usual, delicately balancing the breakfast tray in front of her bosom, she began to scream, more violently and piercingly that one would have given her credit for, with her restrained temperament. All three of them came rushing in, Sabine, Andreas, and Daniel, ready to put out a fire, since it sounded as if the van Lier woman were going up in flames.

He saw his landlord for the first time. A gray, stubble-covered, old man's face that seemed strangely small, with a pointy nose, jaw hanging down, and clouded eyes, of which only yellow could be seen, lying on a white pillow. The colonial official was dead.

"Don't yell like that, you'll have the neighbors on our necks," said Sabine, and this time she was unquestionably right: even the van Lier woman could understand that and stopped right away. She let herself, trembling all over—which resulted in a noisy staccato from her corset—fall into a chair, tore the nickel-rimmed glasses off, and sobbed noiselessly to herself.

Sabine thought they should notify the doctor and the undertaker: "I am, may God hear my lament, an orphan, and know what has to be done in such situations." But the van Lier woman had locked herself in, this time in her own room, and since no one else knew the doctor's address or whether the deceased had left any special wishes for his burial, the notifications were not carried out, which soon proved to be a blessing.

Because Daisy, summoned by Andreas by telephone, in black and hence somewhat alien to her usual self—though no less charming—said, after spending a quarter of an hour alone with the dead man and coming into Andreas's room with eyes reddened from crying, "Well, that's a nice mess. Now what'll we do?"

They looked at her blankly, then what she meant slowly began to dawn on them. None of them had recalled up til now that the lease on the entire apartment expired with the death of the colonial official. Andreas could insist on keeping his room, but then he'd be the sub-tenant of people he didn't know at all.

Without that room, Daniel was lost. Andreas knew that neither of them possessed enough strength to lead the life of many fugitives who switched from one dwelling to another, always on the run, dependent on the good will of total strangers.

He assured them, trying to seem less worried than he really was, that it would be quite simple, he'd just rent the whole apartment himself, and turned over in his mind the amount he'd have to whee-dle out of his mother to come out right. (Getting around the cur-rency restrictions wasn't difficult.) But he was immediately reminded by the van Lier woman that the owner of the building was not about to hand over the apartment, "not even to us and certainly not to a German." If anything, he was impatiently awaiting her employer's demise, had already asked her three times, in the most tactless way, how much longer things could last; he wanted the apartment for his daughter, who, newly married, needed a place to live.

They all became silent. Even Sabine had lost her powers of speech. Daniel stared dejectedly at his hands, a faint smile on his lips, and acted as if none of it had anything to do with him.

Andreas felt helpless, got angry, stood up, took one of the arrows from the wall and snapped it in two. "There," he said and put the pieces in the van Lier woman's lap. Then he sat down again, not feel-ing a bit better.

"We can't let anyone find out he's dead," Daisy said eventually. "We have to get rid of the body."

That didn't sound particularly delicate or much like a loving child and elicited from Sabine the remark, "Things like that are just not done," but Daisy just looked down her nose at her and asked, "Can you think of anything better?"

And since Sabine, of course, couldn't think of anything better, Daisy immediately got busy organizing things. The doctor had to be let in on it, she claimed she could stake her life on him; on the other hand, her husband, who fortunately was away on a trip, must not hear anything about it. He'd stopped visiting his father-in-law, who had accused him of pro-German sentiments.

After various telephone conversations, she said dejectedly, "Can't come up with a car."

She pulled Andreas into the living room and put her arms around his neck. "I'm doing all this for you. It's a terrible crime."

"For Daniel."

"For Daniel, too. But first and foremost for you."

She glanced at the van Lier woman's bed and sighed. He didn't have the slightest amorous inclination, but wasn't entirely certain what would've happened if Miep had not suddenly thrown open the door and said with an awkward bow, "My condolences, Mevrouw Goedhart."

It was unpleasant for him to have been seen so close to Daisy, but Miep looked at them completely without suspicion. "My aunt told me you need a car. I can take care of that. And anything else you need."

The things that were needed—with which she returned that evening—were a roll of packing paper and cord; the paving stones for weighting the body were left down below in the car. Andreas, together with the driver, a theology student, set to work. They lifted the dead man, whom the van Lier woman had dressed in a dark suit and patent leather shoes, with an orange-ribboned medal around his neck, and laid him on the paper that had been spread out on the floor—which, however, turned out to be too small. Then they decided to use the rug. "'S a sin," said Sabine, who looked in every couple of minutes, "such good quality." Suddenly, Andreas had to run out and vomit; when he returned, the colonial official had been rolled up in the rug and tied in.

Daisy kept a lookout on the lower landing of the stairs and Miep watched in front of the entrance as they carried the rug down in the beam of flashlights, the theologian up front, Andreas behind. It was heavy, heavier than it had a right to be. Their shadows wavered back and forth on the wall, floated up and down: the shadows of two thieves with their booty. Anyone who saw them would know at a glance that something fishy was going on. But no one saw them. They reached the car undisturbed. As they were about to stow the rug in the back, they heard footsteps. Stood motionless, held their breath. Two flashlight beams came closer, blue ones, moving up and down, describing circles. "Come on," hissed the student. But the dead man or the rug or the dead man and the rug proved recalcitrant; they shoved and pulled without getting it in. The future pastor cursed. Just as the two flashlights were going by them, they managed to bend the thing in the middle and get it onto the back seat. Andreas's stomach revolted again; he took one step to the side and vomited on the sidewalk. The lights turned around and slowly came closer, rose, fell; his stomach contracted even more violently, produced nothing more; he just retched up bitter gall. Men's voices, in Dutch. "Are you sick, can we help?" "No thanks, I'll be all right." A woman's voice, in broken German: "Drank a little too much Rhine wine." Now it was Andreas's turn to curse. Then the lights finally turned around and quickly moved away. He climbed in, squatted on the floor, his knee bruised by a paving stone. Miep settled in beside the driver and the car started up.

The suspension was bad; after they'd left the city, the car bounced over the rutted country roads and skidded on a thin layer of snow. It was snowing. Bluish flakes were falling slowly to the ground in front of the louvered headlights.

With fingers stiff from the cold, Andreas wrapped so much cord around both stones that they were almost covered with netting. Then he tied them fast to the rug. Murderer's work. His mouth was dry and full of the taste of vomit, his teeth were chattering. It is not permissible to touch death on horseback. It is not permissible to throw a dead colonial official into the water.

To hell with it, why not? Is the alternative any better? A distinguished congregation of mourners, umbrellas above top hats, top hats above serious faces, faces that have taken on a look of mourning on command, hats off for the prayer, Handel's *Largo*, wreaths with and wreaths without ribbons, flowers wired together and stuck into dark evergreen boughs and again: the venerable congregation of mourners, dignified, with starched shirts, the feet of those being addressed shifting back and forth, cold, wet feet, in bed with the flu tomorrow, isn't he ever going to stop, finally the end, the coffin is lowered and three scoops of earth. Are three scoops of earth better than water? Worms preferable to fish?

What do fish do with patent leather shoes? He laughed hysterically.

The car stopped, Miep jumped out; the student stayed in his seat and kept the motor running. The girl looked over the area with her flashlight and waved. He rose stiffly from his squatting position, wrestled the rug out onto the snow, and dragged it along behind him. Miep showed the way to the bank. He gave the dead man a shove and heard him splash into the water.

The girl returned to the car. He stood there. They might think he was praying, but he wasn't praying, just standing there with empty hands and empty head, feeling the flakes, agreeably cool against his burning face.

Chapter 11

H E'D already been in Amsterdam for three days. For three days he had not, with the exception of the trip to the dunes, left the hotel. Three days of memories, three days of attempts to write.

On the morning of the fourth day, he went into the city. In the bright, slightly windy spring weather, everything looked neat and clean—the houses, the flowers, the women. Things were going well, people were cheerful, more cheerful than in Germany; they laughed a lot, gave each other friendly looks; their politeness was relaxed, and they had to bear neither a past they had yet to come to terms with, nor an economic miracle. There were a lot of bicycle riders—not having an automobile did not seem to be held against you here—who flitted skillfully between cars. But still in raincoats, even if of more stylish cut and in various colors. A modest people, in harmony with themselves. They liked the world and the world liked them, that was evident everywhere. The stores were filled with goods—fashionable, cosmopolitain, not provincial like at home. In the bookstores, French, English, and German works were on display. Countless Chinese restaurants, East-Asian shops offering ceramics that elsewhere would be seen only in museums, antiques stores with glassed cupboards, Delft china and tiles, tiles on which animals, people, landscapes were portrayed in blue or in a red that verged into brownish, or with a renaissance pattern in blue and dark yellow that simulated a three dimensional view, second-hand shops in which everything from oil lamps to old bicycle parts could be found, souvenirs, dolls in Dutch folk costumes, wooden shoes, normal sized or incredibly tiny, wooden shoes as broaches, ashtrays, vases, made of china, brass, or even really of wood, schnapps bars and cafes, an unbelievable number of banks, offices of steamship companies, mercantile offices, a ship chandler, a billiard maker, garishly made-up fat whores who laughed from wide-open windows, a truck that delivered fresh kitty-litter and took away the dirty, herring sellers, flower stands, hurdy-gurdies just as they'd been forever and a day. Nothing died out here—the old could persist alongside the new: a dog cart dawdled along, with a fat American car following it patiently through the narrow street next to the canal, without honking.

The longer he walked through the streets and alleys, along the canals, over bridges and paths, the stronger the feeling became that this was where he belonged; it was his city, the only one in which he'd lived. Four years, four terrible years in which everything was contained, the whole of reality. Everything before was prelude, delusion, and deception, hidden behind veils; everything afterward a never-ending, monotonously strummed coda.

This realization jolted his heart, which began to flutter. Things began to swim in front of his eyes. He gasped for breath, looked for a place to stop, sat down on the projecting doorstep of a shop and waited, his eyes shut, until the attack had passed. It didn't last long, but still he felt too weak to get up. Probably it had been nothing more than a lack of circulation to the brain; now the blood was flowing again, he could think, was aware of his situation, looked at himself as if he were another person, with a certain detached interest, without sympathy.

He wasn't afraid, though he was constantly moving along the edge of an abyss, and if there was something that bothered him in his fragile condition, it was this lack of fear. It proved to him how much he differed from the world around him, because fear had become the most dominant, most human of all feelings. It could not be banished from the world by a decree, as Roosevelt and Churchill had tried to do with the Atlantic Charter. It was just as much of a determinant as faith had been in other epochs, the wellspring of life, of art.

He longed for the time of his fear, for darkened streets, the firing of the antiaircraft guns, his room, the van Lier woman, even Sabine's chatter, for hunger, illegality, indignation, for the great pain.

The time when he believed it was important to bear witness, the time of hope for a better afterward, for victory.

Daniel had known that there wouldn't be any afterward, not even for those who had made it through. Daniel's sad smile when someone spoke about the future, Daniel's look of rejection when someone extolled that which was to come.

The seventeen-year-old had been right instead of him, the adult. Not the Jews, not the Germans, but he, Andreas, had lost the war.

He had gone to Germany, just for a few days; his newspaper wanted to discuss things with him. He'd arranged the trip so he could be at home for his mother's fiftieth birthday. The one day with the editors in Berlin (new guidelines, the articles had to be more aggressive, more optimistic, and even more slanted in favor of the Germans) was followed by an overnight trip to Munich that seemed endless. He hadn't notified his parents of the arrival time, so no one was at the railroad station. He wasn't expected so early; when he got to Herzogpark, the living room on the first floor was still being cleaned and he had to fight his way upstairs through the piled-up chairs in the entry hall.

His mother, in a shabby Chinese dressing gown, screamed, "Andreas!" She gathered him into her arms impulsively, in a way she hadn't done since he was a child, and shed a few tears, while he unwillingly laid his head against her breast.

His father came out of the bedroom, in suspenders, "My dear son!" his voice wavered. Two strangers who were laying claim to his love.

He asked for a bath and one was quickly drawn. He felt better in the water. A feeling of being coddled—where else in the world would the water be run into the tub for him, at exactly the right temperature, mixed with an essence smelling of pine needles? He began to sing. As a child he'd always sung in the bathtub, the "Birds' Marriage" and "In the Forest Stands a Tiny Man." Then he let the bathtub thermometer sail between the two streams of water like a ship. Skagerrak and Kattegat: two hard words. His father had taught them to him, with index finger raised—modern pedagogy recommends learning while at play—but the effort had been wasted, he wasn't interested in battles. "The flagship," said his father, "the admiral is standing on it." He looked at Papa full of sympathy. "Don't you know it's a little sailboat? It's sailing to the island of Fitzliputzli."

"Fitzliputzli, Fitzliputzli," he sang to himself. Suddenly he became uneasy. What if something happened in Amsterdam? Ridiculous, everything's gone well for so long. Why should something happen precisely during these two days?

But he remained nervous. His hands trembled as he sat over breakfast downstairs, in the hastily tidied-up dining room.

"Are you ill?" asked his mother worriedly.

"No."

"You look wretched. Surely you're not getting enough to eat."

"I get enough to eat."

"Ach, the war, this *awful* war! Do you think it will last much longer?"

"I don't know."

"It can't last much longer," said his father. "The Russians are done for. And the West has never counted seriously."

His hands trembled more violently. "You think Germany's going to win?"

"But of course. That's really beyond question. We've practically won the war already."

Andreas banged the table, two cups fell on to the floor and broke. "Germany is not going to win!" he screamed in a cracking voice.

"*Les domestiques,*" whispered his mother, "Andreas, *les domestiques.*"

His father had stood up. "Our son is ill. We must call the doctor."

"No, no doctor. I'm completely well."

His father sat down again. His mother was kneeling on the floor and picking up the pieces. "Two Meissen cups," she said, but then lapsed into a shocked silence.

"Do you know what's happening to the Jews?" he asked. It was a desperate attempt to get closer to them.

His father cleared his throat, which he always did when he found himself in an uncomfortable situation. "There are no longer any Jews in Munich," he said, so authoritatively that it would appear the problem had been banished from the world by this pronouncement.

"Why didn't you help them? The house is big enough to have hidden half a dozen people in it."

"Andreas," said his mother, still kneeling. She lifted her hands toward him. It looked as if she had thrown herself on the floor in front of him in supplication. "Think of your father's position."

The latter said impatiently, "Ach, what. Position this, position that. No one could risk such a thing. You're not living in this world, which has long been the case, unfortunately."

His mother: "In Holland he has no way of knowing what is happening in Germany."

His father: "I have never noticed, Andreas, that you have been especially interested in the Jews. At any rate, you've not made any exaggerated claims. But if you do not already know, I'd like to tell you: to take Jews into one's house means risking death. I am not exaggerating and mean it literally: risking death."

Andreas helped his mother up, now that she'd finally finished her crawling around, and took the slivers from her hand. Only then was he sufficiently under control to look at his father.

"And you wouldn't expose yourself to the risk of death? Not even to save the life of another human being?"

"What kind of a question is that? Naturally I would risk my life, in order, for instance, to pull a drowning person out of the water. That goes without saying, of course. But here no one is drowning. The measures taken against the Jews are most regrettable and, for an old democrat like me, difficult to comprehend. But to speak of the necessity of saving someone's life seems greatly exaggerated. As far as we know, they have settled the Jews in several places in Czechoslovakia and Poland, on reservations, similar to those for the Indians in America. Naturally hygienic conditions there in the East are not likely to be the best and will claim some victims, but on the other hand they have so many distinguished physicians—indeed, I should say even more than we do."

Andreas kept quiet. He couldn't even prove to his father that he was deceiving himself. What did he know, himself? The East means nothingness. A presumption, not an argument.

The serving girl brought new cups. They went on eating breakfast.

"How long can you stay?" asked Mama.

"Till this evening."

"Only until this evening?" she said and started to cry.

He stroked her cheek, its withered skin neglected since who knows when, then took her by the arm and went to look at the table with the birthday presents. A little begonia plant with a green crepe wrapper, a bottle of "4711" cologne, a large unattractive leather purse. Father's gifts. From his briefcase in the entry hall he got the dress material he'd brought along for her, acquired on the black market from an acquaintance of the van Lier woman, of good quality, blue background with white polka dots—which he didn't particularly like, but she carried on as if it were a treasure.

"You can't get things like this any longer here. And how I can use it. You couldn't have made a better choice. Thank you a thousand times, my son, I'm delighted, even if I should be scolding you for being such a spendthrift."

He put up with her kisses patiently and mumbled, "I'm sorry it's not more."

After these strained pleasantries an appalling pause occurred, the alarm signal that they were getting close to the truth and would have to admit that they had nothing else to say to one another.

Mama caught herself more quickly than he did and asked, in a tone that one would use on a five-year-old, "Your room, Andreas, don't you want to have a look at your room again?"

They went up to the third floor; his father stayed downstairs. The room looked exactly as he'd left it, without a fleck of dusk, the vases filled with flowers. She waited for a kind word; he couldn't think of anything. In embarrassment she walked over to the picture of Positano and pulled at it, even though it was hanging quite straight.

"How is your work going?"

"I'm not writing anymore."

"What do you mean you're not writing anymore? That's simply not possible."

"In wartime most people do different things than before. I produce newspaper articles."

"But that's still writing," she said with relief. "You express yourself in such a funny way."

"Do you really think so? But I don't know whether I'll ever write again." He never weighed his words carefully in his conversations with her and had just simply come right out with this sentence, too. But after it had been said, he thought it necessary to soften it a little: "And if I do, it'll be different than before."

She looked at him from the side. "You're changed. Have you had some bad experiences?"

"You have bad experiences all the time. There's a war on, after all."

"But not really in Holland. I am so grateful you're in Holland and not at the front."

"To whom are you grateful?"

A deep blush. "To the dear Lord."

"So," he said, "to the dear Lord. I'm not so sure you have reason to be grateful to him."

"What's wrong with you? Are you in love, Andreas? Are you having an unhappy love affair?"

"No. Not what you understand by being in love, Mama. And certainly not unhappily."

"But you do have a girl?"

"Yes, you could say that."

"A decent girl, Andreas?"

"Not a streetwalker, if that's what you mean."

"Tell me"—she brought the sentence out only after swallowing several times—"do you want to marry her?"

"Most certainly not. Besides, she's married already."

She reddened again. "A married woman. You know, I just can't comprehend that. So that's it. Now I understand why you're troubled."

He nodded to her, confirmed her in her belief, and knew he was doing something worse that if he'd told her the truth. But he didn't want to talk about Daniel.

When he said nothing more, she gave up. They went downstairs again, sat around idly. She talked about countless friends who didn't interest him (besides, she'd written about all that), and he answered her questions noncommittally: "Yes, Amsterdam is very beautiful," "No, we're not very popular in Holland," "Mejuffrouw van Lier looks after me very well," "I never see the apartment owner face-to-face, he's quite sick."

Birthday well-wishers came, brought gifts: a ham, sausages, butter, cakes and tarts, everything done up prettily with colored paper, ribbons, and flowers. "How charming that your son has come," "the most beautiful surprise," "how happy you must be, Andreas, to be able to let yourself be fattened up a little at home," "oh, this evening already, that is really such a terrible shame." They didn't talk about the war, acted as if there were no such thing, lived the way they'd always lived, with certain limitations, of course; to the extent that they had sons or husbands at the front, they probably worried some, but none of them seemed really to be suffering. No one rebelled or even had second thoughts about what was happening in the world in the name of the German people, hence in their own names as well. It was grotesque to imagine that these people, whose lack of involvement made them seem like phantoms, would one day be held accountable for everything; not without a touch of sadism, he pictured in detail to himself how these respectable, self-centered, middle-class citizens would have to reap what they had sown through stupidity and indifference.

A strained luncheon, alone with his parents. What was there to talk about? Politics was taboo, love was taboo, his writing was taboo, he'd already told about Holland, they'd all read his articles. (They had been carefully cut out by Mama and pasted in the scrapbook.)

"I'd like to go to the museum," he said suddenly.

"To your gothic madonnas," exclaimed his mother happily, because she'd finally found a connection to the past.

But the museum was closed. "De-accessioned," said his father.

"De-accessioned? That's a word I don't know. Funny words you've invented in the meantime. Death on horseback has been de-accessioned."

"'Death on horseback'?"

"Yes, death on horseback. I never wanted to see anything else. Your gothic madonnas can go to blazes."

His parents exchanged silent glances. Don't argue, said the glances. Our poor son.

"Must you really leave this evening already?" asked his father.

"Absolutely."

"You ought to rest up here at home. We could send a doctor's certificate to the editors."

"No," He noted with horror that he could no longer control his voice. "I shouldn't have come."

Mama already had tears in her eyes again. "I didn't mean it that way," he mumbled.

"The war," she said, "this awful war." But that was just mentioned in passing, she'd already said it once. Mechanically, she pushed her discomfiture off onto an abstract force, about which she hadn't the least inkling.

He felt like showing her this force, as it really was, the dirty war, the naked crime, burned people, scorched earth; knew it would have taken nothing more than telling her about the trolley cars to get rid of her witless composure and put an end to the game of hide-and-seek in which she was indulging (if I can't see anything, no one can see me); but while he was still looking for an effective starting point to quickly and mercilessly smash her naivete, she asked, soothingly putting her hand on his, "Did you bring any dirty clothes along?"

"No," he said, pulling his hand back, and they finished eating in silence.

In the afternoon, there was a tea for the ladies. "Had I known you could only stay such a short time, I wouldn't have invited anyone for today," lamented his mother. But he was glad he didn't need to talk, only to sit there eating cake, drinking tea, and could look out into the garden, which, more than anything else here, was a piece of his childhood. Branches stood out black against the yellowish sky, a fantastic latticework. It would be better to paint it than to write about it; suddenly he felt the urge to be freed from words.

The ladies did not let themselves be disturbed by his reticence and chattered on and on, but Mama glanced at him anxiously from time to time.

How is it possible that these are my parents—blind, godforsaken birds, huddled together in the warmth of their nest, impaled on their contentment? My parents, who sleep in soft beds, dreamlessly, ignorantly, without guilty consciences? Whose mouths are running over with decency, honesty, love thy neighbor as thyself? Who believe what they say, but don't say anything that's hard to believe? It's true my father would jump into the water to rescue a drowning person; he believes cries for help when he hears them, but his hearing doesn't reach very far. He doesn't hear his neighbor knocking on the wall, nor the screeching of the trolleys, nor the hoofbeats of riding death.

He handed the cup to his mother to have it filled again. She smiled at him with her expressionless face, from which the girlish charm— which it had possessed just a few years ago—had completely disappeared. He looked at the other women. They all seemed just as gray, just as expressionless, in Sunday-afternoon dresses that were once luxurious but had since gone out of fashion; not a one was beautiful or even simply attractive. They had still not paid the price for the war, but they had for their lives, had for that compassionless existence, unaware of anything that was going on around them, dedicated to their husband's careers, devoted bed-sharers of just one man for a lifetime (once or twice a week), proudly conscious of their role as mistresses of the house and bearers of children. Having children was the object, so that they in turn could have children; they called that their share of immortality. Things that were necessary: a home, a position (with possibility of promotion), a bank account, connections (wives of colleagues for five o'clock tea), beggars (in order to show benevolence), the dead (in order to be sad), misfortunes of others, a summer vacation, edification through beauty (art is beautiful), national consciousness, the dear Lord (to push responsibility off onto Him), and above all, things to do (to fill up the emptiness).

He, however, needed peace and quiet, that was the prerequisite. Morning hours at his desk, without interruption, no telephone, no people, concentration; how was he supposed to concentrate when someone was sitting behind him in the easy chair, when trolleys were rolling, people being carted away, toward the East, toward the end of the world? Millionfold murder in the air, a swarm of locusts that is eating up people's destinies, even those that he writes down, even those that he thinks up; what can a writer do without destinies? Doubt once again, doubt rains from the sky, drips from the trees, clouds the eyes, rots the lungs. He spits out bloody doubt—besmirched with blood, has he committed murder, are the others committing murder? Is he already unable to distinguish between them and himself? Mankind, you murderers—is he no longer a human being? Has he lost his form, that great talent, gift of the gods who laid it in his cradle? He's used it, made something of it, because talent alone is still nothing, so many throw it away in favor of life; but *he* was ready for any renunciation. Friendships fell apart for lack of time, a walk through the garden was relaxation, but right back to the desk again, the place of his great adventure, writing and reading, even being well read was part of good form. How else do you know how little you know? It wasn't a matter of fame for him. He knew from way back that fame was a flighty thing. Actually it was more like ambition, a breathless sprinting after the conjured-up image of what he'd be someday, what he hoped to be someday. But with the chirping of the locusts, whatever form there was had come apart, and doubt was soaking and softening the pieces as if they were papier mâché. The papier mâché knight, the champion of the word, who wrote himself in as the hero of the play, had fallen from the stage and was disintegrating in the mud.

"My youngest can hardly wait to get to the front," was what he heard coming from the wife of the Professor of International Law, who'd already lost two sons in the war.

He looked at his watch. It was time to leave for the station.

Chapter 12

MANKIND—you murderers. Mankind, you murderers for pleasure. Mankind, you who have contrived the belief that murder is permissible, who drape your fellow murderers with medals, pay them pensions, erect monuments to them, force children to learn their names by heart. For you, bravery is a virtue that can be expressed in numbers, measured by the scalps of slain enemies. You murderers who are too cowardly to admit your pleasure and conceal it behind the name of a god or a race, a people or a leader. You murderers with slogans on your lips, members of animal protection leagues, benefactors of underdeveloped nations, church-goers, nature lovers, art enthusiasts!

Your tear-drenched faces when you come out of movie theaters, your hysterical screams in the stadiums. You falsifiers of history and believers in progress, you successful ones, you betrayers of the spirit. Never does your imagination flower more oppulently than when you are devising tools with which you can murder. How shall one who is nothing more than a human being exist along with you? Must he sacrifice upon your altars? Plunge the knife into the heart of the living?

Birds, headless, without tails—bird corpses. Murdered words. A contribution to humanity.

Mankind—you murderers. Hopeless.

Chapter 13

IN Amsterdam, rain squalls; despite that he went home on foot, the portfolio under his arm. He wasn't in a hurry. For him the long train ride seemed too brief a caesura between the two worlds. His parents were still too near; the botched-up day with them hurt now; why hadn't he done a better job of showing his devotion?

Already dripping wet after just a few minutes, he took his time, stopped in front of display windows that were getting to be nearly empty. Stood at a bar in a pub and drank a glass of schnapps that was called "Oude Klare," but was really ersatz, reacted more irritatedly than usual to the hostile looks, and walked faster along the last stretch to Beethovenstraat. Rang the bell downstairs, long-short-long, a signal he gave on coming home ever since the death of the colonial official. Without waiting until the door was buzzed open, he unlocked it and climbed up the stairs. In the doorway to the apartment stood a blond-haired young man.

Blond-haired young men in other people's apartments were suspicious. Even if they were wearing civilian clothes and leaning against the door jamb in an unmilitary attitude. For a moment, they stood motionless opposite each other. Then the blond started to laugh. His laugh made it evident who he was: Daniel.

"Have you gone crazy?" Andreas shouted at him angrily, grabbing at the wig to pull it off. The boy screamed out, then, laughing all the while, clutched his blond-colored hair.

"What do you think you're doing, getting ready for Fasching?"

"I said right away you'd be mad," called out Sabine, "but of course nobody listens to me. Besides, he's exposing me to danger, too, with his ridiculous playing war."

Daniel looked at her angrily, pushed Andreas into the room, and shut the door in Sabine's face. Miep was standing inside; she ran up to Andreas and kissed him, something she'd never done before in front of other people.

"Don't be angry, please, don't be angry. He just simply can't stand it anymore, sitting around here not doing anything, you can understand that. He's been pestering me for weeks to let him join our group. With his black hair that's impossible, naturally, everyone would know he's a Jew. Blond, he looks nice and German, you have to admit."

He unwrapped her arms from his neck and sat down in Daniel's armchair. Incapable of saying anything, embittered that they'd waited until he was gone, feeling deceived.

Miep knelt down in front of him, propped her elbows on his knees and looked at him imploringly.

"Don't say no. We know you can forbid it. He's your child."

It was astonishing how this little Puritan could find ways of getting around him. He made a vague movement but ended up stroking her head. And from that they both concluded rightly that he wouln't forbid it.

Miep went on and on making sure he was convinced, saying reassuringly that Daniel wouldn't take on any big assignments like attacking offices or blowing up bridges, just desk jobs or acting as a courier from time to time, that wasn't particularly dangerous, at any rate no more dangerous than hiding out—many more of those in hiding were being caught than resistance fighters—and he's gotten a really great set of papers, not imitation but the real thing, only the photo had been changed, it would be the work of the devil if and anyway and for sure and if you looked at it the right way.

Perhaps Miep believed what she was saying; Daniel didn't believe it. He smiled deceitfully, the suicidal smile of an immoralist who is defending the thesis that suicide is impermissible on moral grounds.

Since Andreas realized he couldn't restrain him, he smiled too, and just said, "OK, OK," and "Let's hope you're right."

To the perplexity of having to live among murderers was added the far greater perplexity of having helped prepare the way for this most horrible thing of all, through weakness and yielding. Can't you, if you're a human being, say yes, walk out the door, sleep with a woman, without murdering? Dying had set in; already there was no longer a Daniel surrounded by desert and wilderness; silent rejection as often as he looked at the blond boy. Grease paint to penetrate the creases and smooth them out. The idea of salvation through transfiguration foretold disaster.

The waiting began, the endless waiting for the boy who was sometimes gone during the day, but mostly at night; walking back and forth in the room-cage, strained listening, depression, the sense of being lost, headaches, pains in his gallbladder, in his heart; tablets that numbed him but never brought sleep.

He had forbidden Sabine to enter his room; she was afraid of him and obeyed his instruction. He was unpleasant to the van Lier woman, her every word tormented him; so she came in very little and, if she did, just for a short time. Even that didn't suit him. She shouldn't leave him alone; being alone was horrible.

Sometimes he could read, exclusively in English, it didn't matter much whether it was Shakespeare or Eliot, Dickens or a detective story. The language itself, precise, unsentimental, and rich in nuances, acted like a sedative, better than any tablet.

He had to go on writing his articles, there was no other way. He couldn't afford to be thrown off the newspaper and be called up for a new draft-board examination and run the risk of having to leave Amsterdam.

When Daniel came home, he pulled himself together. The boy didn't need to know about his condition (but he knew anyway; shy glances that no longer begged for freedom but for understanding). They talked to one another in a slightly ironic way, acted as if there wasn't a war on, as if Daniel was doing an ordinary job that tired him out to the point of falling over. He slept a lot, and now and again he screamed in his sleep; the carefully guarded fear broke through. Andreas took him by the shoulder and shook him. He sat up confusedly, groaning, saying unintelligible things; then he came to himself, laughed, and lay back down again.

The constant restraint made them hysterical; hysterically cheerful, but also hysterically irascible. They quarreled about silly trifles, misplaced possesions, a new spot on furniture that was already so spotted, and over and over about things that they agreed on deep inside, about politics or, much more, about its practical application—whether the assassination of an SS leader was justified, for instance, when it cost the lives of hundreds of hostages. Daniel sided with the assassins; he who had poked fun at the war of the dilettantes now talked like his comrades, a crude, soldier's language that showed how obediently they had taken on the oppressor's jargon and his view that human lives didn't matter.

Finally, things went so far that Andreas was glad when the boy went out. Then he didn't need to put on an act any longer and could be as serious and sad as he wished. And one night—Daniel had left the house around seven, in a raincoat, with nothing on his head so that everyone could see the blond hair, the Nordic characteristic that was supposed to disguise the oriental melancholy of the face—one night he interrupted his march through the room and sat down to write.

Alert and intent, he composed line after line, improved, abstracted. But when he stopped, he was still a long way from the end of the poem, which, conceived of as a long epic, was to stretch over many pages. He'd finally decided to give up the requirement of being a witness, to give it up in favor of a truth that he could portray, not because he'd been present, but because he was a contemporary. Fear for Daniel became strength; attachment to another human being gave him the impetus to conjure up war with language alone, without cohesive images—each one of which arose from the other—but using only those that were like individual chunks of a mountain rockslide. (Picasso needed a whole wall for *Guernica*; the self-destruction of mankind couldn't be portrayed in brief.)

When Daniel came home, he'd already fallen asleep; he woke up briefly, smiled at the boy, and went back to sleep. Didn't get up until nearly noon. It was a summer day close to fall. They'd now been together for nearly a year.

He woke his friend. "Let's go for a walk. If you can be seen in the street alone, why not with me?"

In just a few minutes they were out in the open fields. Above them hung the huge Dutch sky, that pale blue sky with its drifting good-weather clouds, in front of them stretched a belt of trees that bordered a road, behind that rose the embankment that extended on both sides into the endless distance.

When they had crossed it, that last obstacle, and had it behind them, there was only sky and earth's surface, arching surface and sky sinking down to it, a huge conjugation, watery blue with pale, yellowish green. Beautiful and comfortless; a landscape that does not help man, a landscape without romance, without cheerfulness and without severity, contourless, measureless, pathetic. A provocation to excess. Every vantage point was in the middle; you went from middle to middle and never got away from the spot.

They were out in the open together for the first time, no longer prisoners within four walls. Even here they kept on with their light-hearted tone, talking about this and that and not about what they thought about all the time, because if anything different had pushed its way into their consciousness, even superficially, they wouldn't have been able to think about anything else but murdering.

Seduced by the unaccustomed freedom, the measureless land-scape, Andreas transgressed his self-drawn boundary. He didn't ask the question that always fell on deaf ears: what do you want to do afterward? He provided the answer himself, provided it in a voice that made it seem as if he were gasping for air while speaking—there was a slight hissing that made the words sound breathless and robbed them of their credibility.

He talked about trips together, to Greece, Italy, Paris; in Paris they'd feel at home, maybe in London, too, but they wouldn't go back to Germany under any circumstances. The anonymity of a cosmopolitain city, a foreign language that would have to be mastered—through which you'd gain perspective on your own, the one in which you write. Yes, to him it seemed like an advantage not to let everyday life strip bare the language in which he worked. It was the costly raw material out of which something new would originate. No more aestheticism, no formalism; language was a tool for digging into the depths, in order to finally bring out into the light that which has been buried, lost to history.

Together they'd find the right words to share with others, and listen to those that others sent to them, until their many voices met in one huge discourse in which nothing would be passed over in silence and which would never end, for their own sakes and the sake of those who were ignorant of speech, for whom they would carry it on.

When he'd finished, he looked at Daniel. But he turned his head away, his expression blank, his jaw clenched; tears were pouring from his eyes.

A senseless image of peace, good only for the junk heap.

The murdering was still going on.

Chapter 14

G ET up from the doorstep and be on your way. His heart was beating regularly now, but a pain shot from the pit of his stomach to his shoulder.

City of pilings, mirror-city, city of circles; a centrifuge that pulls you into the middle, the middle of the city, of life. Here, on the pavement of the large square, he'd seen blood, blood shed in war, for the first and only time, just as it was all over, on the day of the capitulation. In the midst of the pealing of bells and the sound of trumpets blaring the national anthem from the church towers, shots were fired. He was close by, pressed himself against a doorway. When he finally went on his way, they'd already dragged away the two dead men who had been shot down by an SS unit barricaded in a house across the square. Only the blood was still there, two red puddles. How awful, people were saying, such senseless bloodshed, now that there's peace. As if it made more sense to shed blood in war. He wanted to argue, but didn't dare: they would have lynched any German.

Today he would have been able to say it. The war was over so long ago, the Germans fostered tourism and brought money into the country. The rain had washed the blood from the pavement, cleaned it up for the rubber-soled and high-heeled creations of a flourishing industry.

He walked by the city hall where he and Susanne had been married (after endless difficulties, hearings, records, testimonies from Sabine and the van Lier woman, he'd gotten a residence permit—"in honor of our dead, whose cause you aided": Daniel's and Miep's deaths for his papers). The Justice of the Peace gave a lengthy address in which there was a lot of talk about brotherhood, despite which he couldn't quite conceal his amazement that a Jew was marrying a German. Susanne in a raincoat, without a hat, like an impudent boy. Pressed to her breast, in place of the bride's bouquet, her only wedding present, his three books.

They were still poor, and he loved her. Only later did it occur to him that, from the very beginning, he'd confused her with Daniel whom she resembled closely, right up to the eyes.

For at least a few hours each day she created the illusion that he wasn't alone, not condemned to loneliness, confronted by the black, oilcloth-covered notebook in which he wrote his first attempts.

She bore all the privations without complaint. In the illustrated romances from which she got her ideas about the world, poets' wives got along without much money. "Boheme" meant you didn't own a vacuum cleaner and cooked on two burners. For that she acquired the right (everything has its price) to share in the intellectual life of a writer.

He didn't offer her much. (Basically, he didn't offer her anything other than his love in bed, still presuming back then that it gave her pleasure; it took a good long while until he recognized that her excitement was the flawless acting of a frigid woman.)

"Are you writing a new book?"

"Yes," he lied, so as not to disappoint her and because it was easier.

"What's it about?" (Obviously a book had to be "about something.")

"I don't want to talk about it until I'm finished." She lowered her head meekly. She put up with anything if it had to do with his work.

They had only one room. Every morning about nine she left the house and didn't return until two. "A poet needs peace and quiet."

But the peace and quiet didn't help him at all; the more peace he had, the less he could write. (He was still emptying the wastepaper basket himself. Susanne didn't need to know.) The confidence that it would turn out alright without being a testimony no longer existed. And now it was high time to speak out. Books, periodicals were filled with eyewitness accounts. He read them and quickly put them aside. It wasn't the right approach. Every word diminished, rendered innocuous; there were no words for what had happened. Indescribable pain.

That room of his defeats. Plush furniture, wallpaper with garlands of leaves on a dark background. The kitchen in one corner. The garbage bucket that stank despite being emptied daily. The sink with a bowl decorated with flowers, the flowered pitcher, the bucket beside it, with Susanne's hair stuck to the cover. The iron bed, meant for one person, in which they slept together. When the lovemaking was over, the battle for the covers began. Susanne always won. He lay at her side, shivering. Superficial, wearying sleep until morning.

After breakfast, she left. Rain or shine. He didn't ask where. He should have. It was uncivil not to have. Often she came home shivering from the dampness. Then she stood next to the small kerosene heater and looked at him with her round amber eyes. Without reproach, with an impassive face. He never knew which was concealed behind her beauty—depth or emptiness.

They lived on support from charitable organizations and the little bit that Susanne's rich relatives sent from America. Until, one day, money came from Berlin. It was only a small advance, but to them it seemed like a huge fortune.

"We're moving to Munich," she announced. "A German poet belongs in a German environment."

He didn't object, although he knew the business about a German poet was nonsense. If he'd been able to write, the environment wouldn't have mattered. But he hoped that by living among the Germans, he could get behind the mystery of how it had all been possible.

The border was hardly behind them when he was seized by measureless excitement. He was as highly charged as he normally would have been just before starting a new work. The devastated cities heightened this condition.

He walked through Munich. Nothing reminded him that he'd once been at home here; he was a stranger who could not, in the rubble over which hung the smell of decay, rediscover his shining city. Inconceivable that human beings were living here along with rats and cats, in ruins on which grass was growing, rampant weeds on every handful of earth.

Whispers from every corner as soon as he showed up: "coffee, cigarettes." They took him for a foreigner with whom business might be profitable. Now and then he bought something, from a whore, an old man in a shabby fur overcoat, a twelve-year-old boy, a mother with an infant in her arms. Exchanged a few words and tried to read the answer to his question on gray faces. But he learned only about the misery of the present and nothing about the past.

If he wanted butter, American canned goods, cognac, he had to go to the black market in one of the villa districts. Here the merchants were eastern Jews; he found them unpleasant and was ashamed of this feeling. They'd all survived the camps. Had they been Kapos—unscrupulous, turncoat killers—or just cunning, well versed in the tricks that were necessary to make it through? They talked about emigration and their hopes of finding a home in America or Israel. Even *their* faces were silent about the past.

With groceries stowed away in his briefcase, he visited his father, who was lodged in the former maid's room in an eight-room apartment on the Isar, in which twenty-one other people were also living. Papa was sitting on his bed, shivering and complaining. Other residents came to visit and complained as well. Self-pity was their theme. Every day, Andreas got to listen to it for an hour. No one seemed to think he might want to say something, too.

When the hour was over, he stood up. Outside, he could at least get enough air to breathe. Bright winter sky above remnants of walls. The arcades looked like ancient ruins. The outwardly intact Theatiner Church, freed of the buildings that previously crowded it in, spread its baroque splendor.

In the inner city, bustling trade. Bundles of kindling, household goods, books, musical instruments were being transported on push-carts. Beside a white marble statue of the Virgin lay sacks of coal. A one-armed man was looking for cigarette butts. Cripples were every-where. Young men in old military jackets from which the insignias had been removed, women of indeterminate age in kerchiefs, loaded down with rucksacks. Among them, clean and well-fed, Leicas dangling from their necks, members of an easy-going master race, the Americans.

He lived with Susanne in a kind of bunker that bore the name of a well-known hotel. He waved away her remarks about justice evening up the score. She'd made friends with an egg wholesaler. He went along with her once; there was roast pig and champagne for breakfast. During the meal, their host lifted Susanne's hand, over and over again, to a mouth dripping with fat while simultaneously discussing an apparently very important business deal with a young man in a leather jacket. Andreas could hear enough to understand that it had to do with trucks that were going to be sold illicitly in the Saarland. When Susanne mentioned the word Ausch-witz over coffee, he kissed her hand once again and said, "You're much too beautiful to think about that. Let's let byones be bygones."

That's what they all said, those fallen angels of pride, who with diligence and industry were trying to get back on their feet, to have a roof over their heads, not to go hungry anymore. In an unheated cellar, a cabarettist sang, "We want to finally be women again." Shaken, Andreas realized that peoples' distress was so great that they didn't have enough strength to think back over the cause of their misfortune. They were paying for something that they had indeed coveted, but had never actually gotten, and that was more than they could comprehend.

Gradually, his tension relaxed. Susanne built the house, and in the end he was living in Germany just as he would have in any other country.

Sometimes he helped Susanne with business transactions. She could figure things out well and hold her own, but he had more ideas. Without really understanding anything about it, using only his lively imagination, he'd managed a few good coups. Since then, she had faith in him, asked his advice, and had him carry out business dealings for her from time to time. He did it willingly; since he had no connection to money, he negotiated coolly and deliberately, not without pleasure in being able to assert himself in such a foreign world.

If she'd just not tried to meddle in his affairs. One of her favorite words was "contacts." She made contacts with radio station managers and stage directors, publishers and editors. Beauty and wealth made her popular. He sat by quietly most of the time. Susanne threw him reproachful glances, and as soon as they were alone she burst into tears. Vainly he tried to make her understand that all those people bored him and couldn't help him anyway, because he didn't have a single manuscript to offer them. A few remembered his name, but nobody invited him to collaborate.

One day a telegram came from the Principessa in Cologne: "Am happy you're alive, send immediately everything you have in the drawer."

"See, they're waiting for you," said Susanne.

"Where did she get my address?"

She laughed without any sign that she felt guilty. He knew she didn't understand what she'd done to him. Without making any attempt to explain it to her, he telegraphed back: "I have nothing."

"Do not believe you," came the answer. "Implore you not to go to any other publisher."

When he didn't react to that, the exchange of telegrams stopped.

The Principessa did not go running after people from whom she had nothing to gain.

There was a time when she'd said, "You are the most gifted of my children, Andreas."

He bent over her thin hand and brushed his half-open lips across the blue veins and licked her old flesh with his tongue. She uttered a grunt of satisfaction; his tenderness flattered her as much as her praise did him.

How old she really was, no one knew. Ancient, in his view. (Yet she couldn't really be so horribly old; Mario, her youngest son—the friend who'd introduced him to the Principessa—was twenty eight. So, hardly over seventy.) But because of her tiny stature, she seemed so fragile and delicate that she embodied, for him, an age that defied measurement, that was no longer subject to any change. Just as uncertain as the number of her years were her origins. She herself gave vague hints that she was descended from Italian nobility, and occasionally dropped into her conversations: "On our estate in Tuscany, painted by Tiepolo" (was Tiepolo ever in Tuscany? Check it out! He'd made a note to himself, then forgotten it); "In our circles, it was customary that a young girl was never allowed to go out in the street alone"; "Because of my marriage to a Protestant I was dead as far as my family was concerned." But her three sons claimed she was from Ottakring, had been in the ballet, and hadn't been able to read or write before her marriage to an important publisher.

That might have been an exaggeration; in any case, she'd learned and, in fact, so well that she ran the publishing house, at first together with her husband, then, after his death, alone. With her incredible understanding for art, she could sense what was genuine, smell it out even when it was hidden under a pile of manure, and drag it out into the light with her old fingers that were as hard as claws. But when genuine things were no longer to be had in Germany, she just shrugged her shoulders and published the crap.

Her love of money was not one bit inferior to her love of art. Of course, her going along with things had made it possible, now and again, for her to smuggle in an "undesirable" author. Andreas was one of them. The price he had to pay for that was joining the Writers' League of the Reich, which meant astonishingly little to him at the time.

No one at the publishing house spoke of her as anything but the "Principessa," but only her sons and the authors whom she designated the "inner circle" called her that to her face. The others had to call her "Frau Doktor," using the honorary title of her late husband. She, however, used the familiar form of address with everyone.

She dictated her letters (perhaps she really had only learned to read but not to write); her large signature was primitive and overbearing. Even where private affairs were concerned, she used business stationery (yes, even when informing him in the spring of '43 that Mario had been killed on the eastern front). Otherwise, little was heard from her during the war. Every Christmas she sent some of the Nazi kitsch that she was publishing and added to her holiday greetings the admonition: "Keep working, my child!"

Until Susanne contacted her, he'd preferred to keep her in the dark as to whether he was still alive. It gave him a certain pleasure to think that she was in mourning for him; it was right that she was—for her he really was dead.

Then came her two telegrams. Susanne was unhappy about his reaction; she had, as usual, meant well but done things badly and couldn't bring herself to say anything more about it.

A few months later, after he'd attended to a meeting at a bank in Cologne, there were still a few hours until his train left. It was raining. He studied the movie listings, but didn't feel like seeing any of the films. He suddenly decided to visit the Principessa.

The doorman at the publishing house was sorry to inform him that Frau Doktor no longer came to her office. Oh yes indeed, she was still quite active in the firm, but only from her villa. Did he wish to call her there?

Instead of telephoning, he took a taxi. On the way, he regretted his impulse, but just couldn't be bothered to ask the driver to turn around. The house was located near the woods; the war hadn't touched it. It dated from the Wilhelmine era and was just as typical and awful as it had been in his memory. In the front garden, mignonettes were blooming (he hadn't smelled their old-fashioned fragrance since he was there the last time); behind them stood planters with fuchsias. Nothing had changed. No doubt the factotum was still there, the one to whom the Principessa left all the flower arranging—she wasn't interested in the garden. She considered the sun harmful to one's health and preferred to stay in her room.

The maid had him wait in the entry hall. He looked around, while in his thoughts he toyed with the possibility of sneaking away before she returned. The furniture from earlier days was still there, Italian Renaissance, very expensive, scarcely to be outdone in gloominess. Only the pictures had been switched. If he recalled rightly, there had been three or four works by Liebermann, Slevogt, and Leibl ("Good, but not in keeping with the times. If I had to have them around me constantly, I'd die of boredom," was the Principessa's verdict). Now a pair of lovers by Chagall was hanging there, and a woman's head by Picasso, and Feininger's sailboats. He knew them all from the time when they'd been hanging in her drawing room as examples of "art that can speak to us."

The maid came back and showed him in. The room—quite large and papered in black—was dim, its curtains pulled closed, and the few pieces of modern furniture made it look almost empty. Andreas walked through the emptiness toward his objective, a floor lamp that was giving off a soft light; nevertheless he managed to turn his head far enough while walking to see the pictures on the walls. They were *tachistes*, one certainly a Pollock, he didn't know the painters of the other ones. Beside the lamp, but in such a way that her face stayed in the shadows, the Principessa was lying, more than sitting, in a leather-covered easy chair.

Tiny as a child, dressed in something gray and fluttery, she stretched her hand out to him to be kissed. He couldn't bring himself to touch the skeleton with his lips.

"I have not gotten any younger, nor have you," she said with a scratchy voice, withdrew her hand with a jerk, and motioned to a chair. "Sit down. I cannot tolerate people who stand. Why did you stop writing?"

He sat down. "It's no longer fun."

"Fiddlefaddle. Tell that to someone else. I know how possessed you were. You just don't have it any more—that's the real story, my boy. People like you just broke apart against that pack of Nazis. Not I. When I hate, I become stronger. Hate has made me mature."

She giggled to herself, gnomelike, evil.

With a start, he thought: She must be well into her eighties and is talking about maturing.

"It's a splendid time. So much talent. Youth, inconsiderate youth, doesn't give a damn about the past. The things you cried over aren't even worth kicking aside. They're right. The future belongs to them"

Talking was a strain for her. Despite that it gave her unmistakable pleasure. "You don't have a future anymore. Your generation has lost the game. There's us and the young. Not you. You're too weak. Not fit for life. You and my poor Mario. My fortunate Mario. He would have lasted just as poorly as you have. In that case, it really is better not to be here anymore. Don't you envy Mario his death?"

It was an impertinent question which could only be given an impertinent answer. But she wasn't really expecting an answer.

"Strength is part of life. Only very few have it and certainly not the likes of you. You're too sentimental. Sentiment is passé. When you do manage to come out with anything, it's antiquated. You didn't perhaps come here to bring me something?"

He shook his head and thought amusedly that just a short time ago, she'd begged him for something. Now she was getting back at him.

"We can be thankful for that. You should all stop writing, nothing's going to come of it anyway."

She leaned back, giggling. He saw now that the armchair was specially adapted to support her head, similar to a dentist's chair.

"Nobody gives a damn whether you're alive or not. It's astonishing how many have died. Do you know that Roberto is dead, too?"

He didn't know. Roberto was her oldest son. Full of sympathy, he wanted to take her hand, but instead she slapped him lightly on the cheek.

"Spare me your condolences. When you're as old as I am, you don't grieve anymore. At most, you get mad that someone's been stupid enough to get killed. Ran his car into a tree. Like the hero in a bad novel when the author can't figure out what else to do. What kind of fellows are they, that they have to prove their masculinity by driving fast? No marrow in their bones. What a brood I've brought into the world. Mario was still the best. The worst is Luigi. A playboy at his mother's expense. Pah!"

She spat out this sound with the utmost contempt.

"Carries on at the Riviera with movie stars. Plays and boozes. Never reads a book. And a thing like that is the Doctor's and my son. He's not allowed in my house anymore. Of course I could shut off his money, turn it over to trustees, but why should I do that to myself? At my age, getting upset is bad for the health. And I intend to stay healthy for a long time yet. Because I love life."

Giggling and snuffling, she had edged into the light. She was wearing a blond wig over her hair, which he knew was thinned out; her face, masklike from so much cosmetic surgery, was rouged. This is the way American corpses must look in those fancy mortuaries where they play Beethoven or Gershwin all day long.

He thought about trying to escape. Fear paralyzed him. Not fear of the monstrosity sitting opposite him, but elemental, irrational fear.

"What are you doing with yourself?" she asked and sank back into the shadows. "Things don't seem to be going badly for you. You look quite respectable. Do you have a rich wife?" Again, he didn't need to answer.

"No wonder things are going well for you. They're going well for everyone. If one of you is unable to earn anything, there's always someone handy by from whom you can get it. Even my dear Mario would probably have married somebody rich. The only thing your generation is any good at is sleeping with heiresses. There are worse things, you don't need to get all red in the face, rich heiresses are generally well bred and well behaved. Roberto has left me with a little bourgeoise with a Saxon accent. *Orribile!*" And this person expects me to take care of her children. As far as I'm concerned, diapers are the most repulsive thing in the world."

"Diapers?" he asked. "So Roberto's only been dead a short time?"

"Diapers in the figurative sense. Don't be so thickheaded. Earlier you were always quite intelligent. Roberto's accident was three, no, wait, four years ago. And now I'm supposed to play the loving grandmother. Da-da and ay-ay. Pah!"

She had stopped laughing. Pushed back still further in the chair, she said with a hard voice, "I pay for them. I have to pay for all of them. Because they're too lazy and incapable of taking care of themselves. I run the publishing business with the help of strangers. Roberto's oldest is sixteen. He could be starting already. Instead of that, he wants to be an atomic physicist. Blow the world to smithereens. Let him, if he'll get any fun out of it. Do you have children?"

This time she really was waiting for an answer.

"Finally I'm getting to hear something reasonable from you. Children are awful. At least the ones that hang on you like leeches. I have the other kind. My good boys. Yes, there's a girl among them, too, but women writers are an abomination. Women in general. Unfortunately she's so talented that she brings in more than all the boys put together. But in wit and esprit she can't keep up with them. Says this lyrical cow to me recently: 'Your boys are in a blind alley, honored Frau Doktor. What they're doing is just playing. That, the cabbalists knew how to do better.' I'd have liked to throw her out, but, may God hear my complaint, she's simply too valuable. So fresh. Just because she wasn't invited to write *Exercise* with the others, now she's gotten her back up. Do you know *Exercise*?"

"No."

"It's over there, lying on the table. Go get it." He was delighted to be able to get up, stretched out the walk to the table (only four steps, but you can actually make something out of four steps), stopped, picked up two black notebooks, *Exercise I* and *Exercise II*, and was about to page through them standing at the table when the Principessa commanded: "Come here!"

Obediently he came back (he succeeded in taking six steps, an improvement) and sat in his old place.

"Read!" she said, but all he could do initially was look—they were sight poems. The words were stretched out across the page diagonally, divided according to neither the dictionary nor phonetics, some were arranged in circles, partly typeset, partly done with a typewriter, and because he was familiar with all that from his own experiments, he was moved and amused. What he read bored him. He couldn't accuse the girl writer of being wrong when she called it playing. What wasn't? And why shouldn't the boys be playing? Playing is better than faking. He'd given up condemning things that he couldn't even get started with himself.

While he was still reading, he heard a sound. A young man had entered the room with the quiet impressiveness of the star who makes his accompanists stop where they are and the audience break out in applause. He was so sure of his effect that he did nothing to heighten it, if you ignored the fact that he was brandishing a copy of *Exercise*. He was tall, blond, poorly combed, and had a nobly drawn face—which, however, was blemished by some sort of excess (it could even have been an intellectual one). Probably this is the way a young girl imagined a poet nowadays, provided, of course that she didn't discover the evil that radiated from him. But then it could be, too, that evil would fit into her picture of a poet as well.

He quickly walked over to the Principessa (he needed only three steps from the table), bent down over her hand, brushed his half open lips across it and then bit down forcibly, which elicited a cry of sensual pleasure form her. After he let go, he said, "Principessa mia, did we spend a pleasant night?"

"Sleepless, as usual."

"Poor, dear Principessa."

When she introduced Andreas, to whom he'd paid no attention at all, he scarcely turned his head and said, in an unfriendly tone, "Delighted."

Suddenly he wrinkled his brow. "Didn't you use to write? Latter-day expressionism or some such thing. But that doesn't make any sense. You can't really be that old."

The Principessa squeaked with pleasure.

"You've been forgotten. How quickly that happens when you don't deliver what you promise."

Then she became, as he'd often seen earlier, a solemn priestess, stretched out her arm and announced: "Jeremy Schluck."

Obviously, everyone knew Jeremy Schluck. When Andreas didn't react, she added, "The most gifted of my children."

He didn't know whether she remembered that she'd called him that, too. Was it a direct effront or just coincidence? But what her "You're not fit for life" had failed to achieve, this statement did.—It hurt.

Jeremy Schluck saw that and smiled.

"Most Honored Lady," he said, "we need to get down to business.

I have to give the Laudatio at the award ceremony this evening. And tomorrow a lecture before the Kant Society. Of which I have not yet gotten a word down on paper.

Now Andreas smiled, but Schluck said menacingly, "On paper, dear sir, in my head the lecture is already perfected, obviously. One has to fulfill his obligations. You guys were worse poets, of course, but you had a basically simpler life. Not this rat race. Whoever can't keep up the pace doesn't count. So we keep up the pace."

He laid the black notebook on a red pillow he'd pulled out from behind Andreas's back and handed it over to the Principessa.

"*Exercise trois,* your Grace. With a plea for the greatest possible benevolence."

She took it beamingly and paged through it, slowly at first, then faster and faster. From what Andreas could see, it consisted of a partially regular, partially irregular sequence of black and white pages that were empty.

Nervously she held it under the lamp, then began to complain: "My eyes. My poor eyes. I truly did not know they're so bad. I can't see a thing anymore without glasses. Jeremy, my dear, go over into the study, they must be lying on the desk."

Jeremy doubled up with laughter.

"Principessa mia, your incomparable eyes are as good as ever. You are seeing correctly. The pages are empty."

She looked as forlorn as a schoolgirl who hasn't done her homework. Vainly, she tried to discover in Jeremy's face whether he meant it seriously or was only joking. He was looking straight ahead with a stern expression and avoided saying anything to her.

Finally she began to feel her way along.

"Is the book finished? Is it to be published as is?"

"Of course, Altezza, what else?"

Then she clapped her hands with pleasure.

"Ach, you wonderful, brazen children. Get the people to pay and send them home with empty pages. Provoking the bourgeoisie. Absolutely right, you dears, you're on the right track."

Jeremy Schluck gnawed at his lower lip, his nose twitched up and down, rabbit-like. With a brutal motion, he grabbed the book from her hand.

"What a horrendous misunderstanding. We're not out to provoke. We have devised *Exercise trois* as a pleasure for people. These sequences of black and white are composed rhythms, they are intended to—and will—stimulate the imagination. We are not manufacturers of finished products, we deliver the materials that force people to do their own thinking. That's what counts. Enough of that ready-made stuff, enough of this dependency on others. Everyone's a poet. If someone doesn't know how to get started, that's just too bad."

Jeremy was serious about it. Perspiration stood out on his forehead. He and the others whom he meant by "we" had discovered that you can turn water into wine.

Dead end or way out? Andreas couldn't decide. He was impressed and revolted. A new world. Empty of history. Our history, the history of murdering, has become empty of objects. Black and white pages. Movement and rhythm. A primordial beginning after too much that has been.

The glassy, old eyes of the Principessa looked around irresolutely. There was twitching around the surgically tightened mouth. Any second she was going to start to cry.

Did he know her so poorly? Her claws balled into fists. With colossal effort, she let out a short, croaking scream. Jubilation that sounded like despair.

"You wonderful children," she stammered, being careful not to say the wrong thing again, "to you belongs the future. Come here, my Jeremy, I want to kiss you."

Then Schluck let himself down on one knee and bent his head so far forward that she couldn't reach anything but his forehead with her lips.

Even a kiss was too much for her. With a soft groan, she lay back. Jeremy took her hand into his mouth and sucked on it.

Then he whispered, "Principessa mia, your poor child has debts. I need money."

Unnoticed by the other two, Andreas left.

Chapter 15

N o," he said.

"Yes," he said.

"No," he said, and then, finally, "Yes."

Because he'd said yes, he was now lying on a couch, hearing a voice behind him: "Just say anything that comes to mind."

"In your waiting room there's a gothic madonna, not anything very good, I think it's a nineteenth-century copy. There's an abstract painting hanging across from the madonna—not a copy, but it's no good anyway. You don't seem to know much about art. On the round table are three magazines. Culture for the household. I leafed through them. They all show gothic madonnas and abstract art, along with villas that are full of gothic madonnas and abstract art. Around your circular table are five Empire chairs. Clunky and uncomfortable. Is it intentional, that your patients have to sit uncomfortably before they come in to see you? Do you think discomfort helps concentration? With me that's not the case. Discomfort irritates me, when I'm irritated I can't concentrate. And why are there five chairs? Why not six, which would at least create a certain symmetry. Three would be OK, too, three is a sacred number and strongly symbolic. Why exactly five? You only see your patients by appointment, each session lasts an hour. So it's unlikely that several people are going to show up in your waiting room. Do whole families come to see you? Parents and three children? And what happens if there are four children? Must one of them sit on the mother's lap then? They might be grown-up children. A difficult situation. So why the five chairs?

"Go on talking," said the man behind him. "Whatever comes into your head. That was a good start."

"You ought to have your ceiling painted. It's dirty. Probably you've never lain here. Try it. It would help convince you to have the painter come. How would it be in another color? Deep red? They know all about such things these days. Deep red generates warmth and comfort. Don't you need warmth?"

He paused, but received no answer. "Are you impolite on principle?"

Again a pause, again no answer.

"So you insist on a monologue. What will you do if I don't go on talking?"

"I'll wait."

"How much do you get per minute for waiting? My wife agreed on the price with you, but I'll bet you're very expensive. My wife only goes in for things that are expensive, she firmly believes that what's expensive has to be good, too. Maybe you *are* actually good. Women probably flock to you. You're good-looking, a gentleman with graying temples, a man of the world who can afford to run around in a corduroy jacket and open shirt. I'll bet you know how to pronounce St. Moritz the right way and where in the whole world you can eat the best lobsters and the best steaks, and think that anyone who has any respect for himself stays at the Danieli and Villa Igea. It's not impossible that you go big game hunting in Africa. You certainly must love to lecture and speak a lot at medical meetings."

Tired out, he remained silent. His head was too low, but it was too much trouble for him to ask for another pillow. The man behind him didn't move; only his soft breathing was to be heard. An unsympathetic breathing. Annoyed by the silence, he started to talk again.

"In front of a butcher shop in Tetuan there were four horse's legs, cut off at the fetlocks."

He knocked the pillow away, perhaps it would be less uncomfortable to lie completely flat. The oriental rug that lay on top of the couch scratched the back of his head. He fished around for the pillow, squashed it together, and shoved it behind his neck. The voice said, "Keep on talking."

"When do you turn on the spotlights?"

No answer. A match was pulled across the striker and flared up. The man behind him lit a cigarette.

"Are you going to put the lighted cigarette against my forehead?"

A chuckle. "Keep on talking. Whatever comes to mind."

"Injections of air into the veins are just too inconvenient. I don't expect you have a syringe in your hand."

"That's a very pretty complex you have there," said the voice. "Presumably not your only one. We'll see."

Outside, far away, a trolley car went by. He jerked, pulled his legs up. Unable to straighten them out again.

"Relax," ordered the voice.

After several attempts, he succeeded in unbending his knees. He lay flat again, but his muscles were still in spasm.

Then he made an abrupt movement to sit up. Two hands on his shoulders pushed him down again.

"Stay lying down. Go on talking."

"Four cut-off horse's legs with hooves."

Nothing else came to mind.

"In Tetuan," the voice prompted him.

He pressed his lips together, shut his eyes.

The man behind him waited. Breathed. The silence was frightful. He knew he wouldn't be able to stand it very long. He pulled his legs up and hoped for the order to relax. But nothing happened. After a while he gave up.

"My wife, who likes to travel a lot more than I do, is afraid of the native quarters. Trauma from the camp, maybe. She hates dirt and despises cripples. Because of that she didn't go to the casbah with me, she took the car and drove to the ocean to swim. It doesn't bother her a bit to go driving twenty or thirty kilometers through Africa alone. She's quite courageous. Her fears are limited to certain things."

A fly landed on his nose; he chased it away with his hand. The next moment it was back again and the sequence was repeated.

"Go on," said the voice.

"Have you ever been in a casbah?"

"In Tangiers."

"That's not a real one. Too many Europeans, too many tourists. In Tetuan I didn't meet up with any Europeans."

The fly again. He slapped at his forehead without hitting it.

"Go on."

"In the beginning it seemed like you could take it all in at a glance, in one bazaar sat the shoemakers, in another the tailors, in a third the spectacle-makers, in the fourth the basket weavers. No one was buying much, people were walking around, talking, walking on, talking some more, walking again, busy in a gloomy sort of way, obviously not very happy about just standing around doing nothing, so many of them that it seemed impossible for anyone to be left at home, all of them in rags, most of them with inflamed eyes with pus dripping out, a lot of them blind. Horrible skin diseases, faces eaten away, fanatically showing their deformed limbs. They looked right throught me as if I were glass."

The fly landed on his upper lip. He closed his mouth. It flew up and crawled across the gray ceiling. He was sweating, pulled his handkerchief out of his pants pocket and wiped his face. Although the pause was long, the voice said nothing.

"It would have been easy for them to do away with a European. No one would find him. I didn't have anything against being killed, so I kept on walking."

The fly was no longer crawling; it was sitting still, a dark point. Ready to swoop down on him. He stared up at it.

"Farther and farther, toward the hills where there aren't any more houses, only huts and caves. A few miserable stores. Hardly any people. In front of a butcher shop, the horse's legs. Cut off right at the fetlocks, the brown hair smeared with blood. They weren't standing in a row, but just like they belonged to a living animal. It nauseated me. I'd never seen anything that horrible. Not in my entire life. Never."

Shrilly, although the man behind him hadn't said a thing.

"Instead of running away, I stopped. Noticed, next to the horse's legs, pressed against the wall, a boy in a ragged brown burnoose. The hood covered his hair. He was holding his hand outstretched, bent into a cup, motionless; nothing but that hand indicated that he was begging. I took out all the change I had in my pocket and put it in his hand. It didn't close, just stayed outstretched. The boy had inflamed eyes, though without pus. For a moment I thought he was blind. But then I realized that he was not staring through me like the others, he was looking at me."

The fly had flown down from the ceiling and was buzzing around his face. He hit at it with his handkerchief. It landed on the brownish wallpaper.

"He looked like Daniel. They all did. But he even more so."

"Who is Daniel?" asked the voice.

He was astonished that Susanne hadn't mentioned him. "He doesn't have anything to do with this."

Suddenly he turned around and hit the wall with the flat of his hand. The fly stuck there, a black spot.

"I'm sorry," he mumbled, "your wallpaper."

"It's washable," said the voice, "go on."

"The coins were still there in his hand. 'Sorella,' he whispered. When I didn't understand, he said again, louder, 'Sorella.' Now I understood—he was offering me his sister. I shook my head. The he let the coins slide into his burnoose and took me by the hand. I didn't resist. Why? I don't know."

"Desire for adventure?" said the voice.

"No. Certainly not that. More likely the resemblance. Daniel, with infected, almost dead eyes. The same facial structure, the same narrow, slightly bent nose, the same brown, very long hand."

When his legs went into spasm, the man put his hand on Andreas's forehead. A strong, very masculine hand that smelled of cigarettes and lavender. It had a calming effect. "Go on," said the voice.

"I let myself be pulled along. Only a few steps to the entrance of a hut. We came into a dirty room, in which, besides two chairs, there was only a bed with a horse blanket. The floor was of clay. The hut had no windows, the light came through the curtain of black glass beads in the doorway. A girl was squatting on the bed. She stood up immediately, a child of twelve at most, in a gray, European smock, a kind of school uniform, only the white collar was missing. She looked like Daniel too, even more than her brother, because her eyes were healthy. Without a word of greeting, she slipped off the smock and was naked. She had a sweet child's body with the first suggestion of breasts. I stepped back. 'Bella,' said the brother approvingly. 'Bellissima,' I answered, agreeing with him, although I was convinced he didn't understand the step up to the superlative. He said something in Arabic, it must have meant something like 'please!'—'No.' He got that. 'Non dormire?' he asked disappointedly. Then he smiled and said, 'Vedere.' Probably these were the only Italian words he knew, they'd been taught to him for the purpose. Not until this moment did I understand what I'd gotten myself in for, and waved my hand to say no."

He pulled up his legs again. "Can I have a cigarette?"

"Anything that helps you relax."

The cigarette was put into his mouth, again a match traversed the striker and flared up, hovered above his head. When the cigarette was lit, the hand put an ashtray beside him.

He inhaled the smoke.

"Go on," said the voice.

"I waved 'no' but stayed. Now the boy was naked, too. Very slender, very beautiful. He pushed a chair over to me, walked behind his sister and put his arm around her, covering her hint of a breast with his hand. I should have been revolted by it—two children, brother and sister, performing the *ars amandi* for me, standing, kneeling, lying, sometimes he on top of her, then she on him, caresses with the genitals, the mouth, the hands, refined holds, double-jointed acrobatics, but everything quite light, entirely dance-like, neither crude nor vulgar. One can't really describe it and I don't expect you to believe me."

"Why shouldn't I believe you?" asked the voice, unexpectedly soft.

"Everything went according to certain rules, rehearsed like a ballet, elevated, artificial. It was art, in fact a perfect sort that I've never seen before or since. Their slender, brown bodies gleamed, they let out cries. I was convinced that they loved each other despite all the carefully drilled show and were enjoying it greatly."

He closed his eyes, hoping he'd be allowed to sleep now, but the voice, cold and demanding again, said, "Go on."

"I don't know how long it lasted, I was carried away, enchanted, intoxicated; it had nothing to do with sensual pleasure, I had no desire for these two and didn't forget for a moment that they were children. I was aware of the most horrible degradation as well, but the amazing thing about it was exactly that everything came so close together here, the borders got blurred, beautiful was ugly, ugly was beautiful."

He turned his head to the wall and stared at the spot. In with the black was a little red, a tiny drop of blood. He breathed heavily, spoke with difficulty.

"So hypnotized that the children were gone and in their place was Daniel, Daniel and another Daniel. The two Daniels were making love, they would beget a third Daniel, I was sure of that. Daniel, the immortal, had come back, the world was intact again, without murderers, free for the word, for my word."

He sobbed audibly, then went on speaking calmly.

"At some point they finally let go of each other; the sister slipped into her smock, the brother tied on a loincloth and looked at me questioningly, to see if I was satisfied. I nodded and reached for my wallet, ready to give them everything I had. But the wallet was gone, lost, stolen, I don't know which. I tried to explain to the boy with sign language. He looked at me without any indication that he understood. 'Domani,' I said, 'ritornero domani.' No good. He held out his cupped hand again. 'Domani,' I said in desperation, 'domani, morgen, manana, demain, tomorrow.' Nothing worked. His sister came over, held out her hand, too, and mumbled beggingly. Their eyes begged. Daniel's eyes. And I couldn't give them anything."

"The children had probably stolen your wallet. An old trick," said the voice contemptuously.

"No!"

He wanted to turn around, was restrained. "Go on."

"The two hands stayed outstretched. 'Soldi!' said the brother. 'Sooooldi!' sang his sister after him. 'Domani, non oggi, domani.' Their refusal to understand made me impatient, the spell was gone, I already knew that even this hadn't helped at all. I felt like hitting them, knocking some sense into them. Stupid little animals that couldn't comprehend anything. Suddenly the girl's brown hand, with its dirty nails, shot out toward my breast pocket. When he saw that, the boy began to feel around my rear pants pocket. They jumped up on me, searched me, spewing out Arabic words—it sounded like an angry quarrel between monkeys. I hit out around me; they were quicker, more agile. If I managed to shake one off, the other was hanging on me again, but most of the time, both of them, they pulled my hair, scratched my face, and howled because they couldn't find anything. Then they saw something that attracted them. The sister bit down on my hand, and while I was screaming with pain the brother tore my watch off my wrist. It was Daniel's watch. Every night before he went out, he put it down on the table beside his bed, and ever since he failed to return I've worn it. I tried to take it back from them, but it didn't work, the two of them were too much for me. But I finally got both of them away from me for a second by kicking them and used that moment to get away. The sister chased me into the street. I ran as fast as I could, then a horse's leg whizzed by me. The second one hit me on the back of my head; the hoof must have cut the skin—there was a dull pain, I felt around with my hand, it was covered with blood. I ran and ran, with my handkerchief pressed against the wound. After a while, I looked around—no one was there."

He pushed the pillow away. The cover still scratched, but he didn't do anything more about it. Dead tired, he stretched out.

Then the hand tapped him on the shoulder.

"The hour is up. You can go. Tomorrow at the same time. You're a patient who cooperates well, I wish I had more like you. Don't forget to write down your dreams. Dreams are especially important to me."

When he stood up, the doctor was gone. A blond girl in a white uniform helped him into his overcoat. "No," he told Susanne at home. And it stayed no.

Chapter 16

———

CITY of mirrors, city of windows.

City of reflections, of recurring images, thrown back by the water, thrown back by the windows, an eternal tennis game with images, back and forth, without ever tiring. Match point only when the sun goes down.

Then it's time to walk past the whores who are luxuriously enthroned behind windows, to walk to the Zeedijk, the sailors' street, to drink a beer and let yourself be convinced by the coalescing sounds of all those languages that *now* is no longer *then*.

Perhaps there will be someone with whom he can talk about things, some person who's listened to the confessions of Camus' heroes, but naturally he manages to go into the wrong bar.

No one was there except a male couple, one man about fifty years old who looked as if a wife and children were waiting for him in some small provincial town, and a young man with penciled-in eyebrows and bleached hair, a bored, cellar-child who was smoking a cigarette and affectedly stroking the hand of his admirer; only after he'd been given a coin and turned on the jukebox did he come out of the lethargy of boredom and fall into the lethargy of rapture, with dissolute eyes, light swaying of his body, and a blissfully idiotic smile on his face.

The barkeeper sat behind the counter reading a newspaper, obviously intent on not being further disturbed by his patrons, now that he'd grudgingly served them. He looked like a grade school teacher, thin, wearing glasses; a pennypincher with his sights set on higher things.

Curled up in a chair lay a fat, gray angora cat; around the counter crept a smooth-haired, tan dog with beautiful, expressive eyes, but nervous and shy and just as emaciated as his owner. After a while, he stretched out in a dark corner, his head on his paws.

But the gentleman who could have heard his confession wasn't there. There was no such person, Camus had invented him, he was the artistic creation of the writer. In reality people aren't used to spending a lot of time listening to the story of some unknown person. True stories are boring; we have television, the movies, the soccer stadium —that's life. If you want to confess, turn Catholic.

He didn't even really want to confess, couldn't, he hadn't done anything. Doing nothing can be more evil that doing something, but what should he have done? What else besides wait?

Wait, get up, walk around, stand at the window, sit down, drum on the table with your fingers, scrape your nails across the glass, press your forehead against the wall, light a cigarette, take two drags, put the cigarette out again, look at the torn painting, play chess with yourself, always the same game, if black wins, everything will be OK, if white wins there'll be trouble, but every time it ends in a draw, throw yourself on the bed, get up, wait.

Say "Dear God" without believing in god.

Burn the poem that he's finished the night after the walk through the fields. The night before the morning when Daniel doesn't come home at the usual hour and when waiting becomes focused on fulfillment again, for the last time, and with an intensity such as never before.

Then it becomes an end unto itself. He waits, but no longer for Daniel; Daniel won't come. Daniel is in prison, has been caught, along with Miep, printing an underground newspaper.

Go on waiting anyhow. Without sleeping, almost without eating. Rack your brains over what can be done. You have to be able to talk to those people. Scream at them: "Don't do that! You can't do that!"

They're not so stupid, so indifferent, so low, that there are no words with which to reach them. But they are. But you have to, you have to…

Unraveled hours. Valuable time lost. Have to risk an attack on the prison, free Daniel, run away with him. Or die along with him. Put your own life on the line. Throw a bomb into the central command post. Make an assassination attempt against Hitler. You have to, you have to…

Instead of that, you send clothing to prison, woolen blankets. Nothing else is permitted. Miep's mother takes them. "The warder," she says, "was very friendly. A good man."

She looks quite happy. Miep is among good people.

Waiting again. Being alone. This failure to comprehend that you have to be the same person for your whole life. The intense desire to be several people.

Curse the stupidity, the awful dilettantism of the resistance.

"Foolish carrying on," says Sabine. "Pinpricks to the enemy. Completely ineffective. And for that, such a clever boy is trading his life."

"Stupid goose!" he screams violently, "Get out!" She takes a frightened jump to the side and shuffles away, shaking her head. He bangs away at the wall with both fists. Unjust, like the others.

Three steps forward, three steps back, three steps forward. He could go out. But he doesn't want to. Because he's afraid of the light, of sounds, of people.

Daisy knocks on the door: "Open up."

He rolls up into a ball on the bed, lies there without moving. His forehead is moist.

"I have to talk to you."

The knocking becomes louder.

"Andreas!"

"No."

"Andreas, darling—"

"Go to hell."

She cries, then he hears her going away and is calmer for a short time. But then comes the silence and when it's quiet he begins to wonder. Always the same thing: What is Daniel doing at this moment? The desperate desire to know, the anger because he doesn't know, the constant identification, he is Daniel, Daniel is he; since he doesn't know what Daniel is doing, he no longer knows anything about himself, is lost in the silence, in the room, prey to his raging imagination. Everything that can be connected with imprisonment—from the arenas with wild animals in ancient times, to the torture chambers of the middle ages, to the electric chair—becomes reality. An old picture of a man with a lead ball chained to his leg, jails from American films, high-technology circular structures and bars that cut faces into pieces, Kafka's penal colony, Edgar Allen Poe's pendulum slowly swinging down on the prisoner, lead walled prisons in Venice, the watery cells of Chillon, the mortuary, and, most often, the man in handcuffs, flanked by two grim-faced policemen, whom he'd seen as a child.

Meanwhile, black says check, white covers with a pawn, after four moves it's a draw. He sweeps the figures off the board with his hand, but the desire to see black win is so strong that he immediately sets them up again. And the game starts all over.

He hardly thinks of Miep. No one needs to be afraid for her. She'll get a few years in jail. Maybe five. But the war can hardly last five years.

But what will happen to Daniel? Soon the dark hair will grow back. If they don't already know he's a Jew.

They do know. Daniel has admitted it at the first interrogation. The tom-toms of the underground movement that beat in the thickets of the city tell of it a few hours later. But about the reason for his confession, the drums say nothing. Was he tortured? Did they give him drugs? Was it his pride that drove him to this statement, his longing for death? Nothing but questions without answers. There will never be an answer.

Two English sailors came in, but when they saw there were no girls there, they left again. The barkeeper shot a venomous look after them.

Suddenly the young man stood up, as if pulled by strings, and began to dance. With his lower body protruding, he thrust his hips first to the right, then to the left, raised and lowered them, swung them in a half-circle, practically dislocated them in a squat, clapped his hands, and clicked his tongue in rhythm. His friend was embarrassed, wanted to pull him back to his chair, but couldn't grab hold of him; for a brief time he ran awkwardly after the cleverly evasive movements, then gave up, shook his head as if to indicate that he didn't condone this youthful craziness and emptied his glass in one gulp, as if to emphasize the point. The frenzied rhythms continued to pour from the garishly lighted glass box; it was enchantment, bewitchment. The young man's face was moist, he uttered sobs of ecstasy, mascara ran down his cheeks, his hair hung down across his forehead, there was pain mixed in with the entranced smile, he looked like someone dying. Soon he was going to fall over, but no, he was still swinging his hips and clapping his hands, gone berserk, about to storm into the void armed only with his paltry body. When the device had finally produced its last sound, he shrieked and fell to the floor, but was on his feet again immediately, then staggered over to his chair, and put his bleached head on the shoulder of the other man, who wiped the mascara off his face with a handkerchief.

Loud howling echoes through the apartment and after being startled out of bed, he runs from his room toward the horrible screams, finds the van Lier woman stretched out on the colonial official's bed, a quivering mass of flesh from whose depths the same words are coming over and over again: "Miep, our little Miep."

He bores into the flabby mountain with his hands without putting a stop to its quaking. She goes on screaming, then finally sits up ponderously. Her corset creaks and groans, she gropes around for her nickel-rimmed glasses which have disappeared in the folds of the blanket.

When she looks at him with her naked, distressed eyes, he thinks he know's what's coming; in a second it'll come gurgling out that Miep has been sent away from Holland to a German camp. But she says clearly and distinctly, "Shot as a hostage."

His head swirls, he leans against the bedpost, slowly sinks to his knees.

"A child, that can't be, she's just a child!"

The Germans have shot a child.

He takes the van Lier woman's hands and presses them together: "Daniel?"

"Not Daniel. My sister has seen the list."

Not Daniel! A feeling of triumph, as if he were the one who'd prevented Daniel's being there.

When the Mejuffrouw has composed herself somewhat, he sits with her in the living room and patiently listens to her speculations about Miep's death. "She didn't cry," she insists over and over again, "that I know for sure, I know her that well." No, he doesn't believe so, either. "If for no other reason, so as not to appear cowardly in front of the Germans. Even those criminal gunmen must have had respect for this Dutch girl who let herself be shot without tears. Because she did not cry." For the umpteenth time he agrees: "Absolutely not." The thought of not crying has a calming effect on her that he can't fathom. "What would she have thought about, the poor girl?" He shrugs his shoulders and says that nobody can know that and it's not proper to go asking about it and mumbles something about the solitariness of dying. But she's not listening to him, and goes on in the same vein and summons up a picture of romantic heroism in which there is no fear and no being at someone's mercy, in which being shot becomes a sort of gymnastic exercise where one is led out in disciplined rank and file and, in the end, is lying motionless on the ground. "She did not cry. She stood there erect, refused to have her eyes bound, and fell with the cry: 'Long live Holland!'"

And this version catches on eventually, becomes legend; one person tells it to the next, the tom-toms pick it up, drum it throughout the city, throughout the whole country. After the war, it will be there in the schoolbooks to be read about, the story of the girl hero, the Dutch maiden who died, bravely and without crying, for the freedom of her fatherland.

The boy, who'd been dozing for a while, had awakened again and whispered something to his friend. The latter shook his head and rapped angrily on his glass, at which the barkeeper folded the newspaper, walked over to the table, and said in an unfriendly tone, "One-eighty." But the man from the provinces didn't want to pay at all, he wanted another beer. The barkeeper brought it, went back to his place behind the counter, and went on reading his newspaper.

At the same time, the dog had gotten up too, followed in his master's footsteps, his hungry gaze fixed on the men. When he saw that nothing was going to be thrown down to him, he went over to the cat, which squinted, hissed softly, and batted him across the nose with its paw. With his tail tucked in, he shrank back, and crawled away into his dark corner. The cat licked off its paw, rolled up into a ball, and went to sleep. For a while, nothing happened. Then the boy persuaded his suitor and was given another coin; with the victor's quick step he walked over to the juke box and gave a kick to the dog that was standing in his way, wagging its tail. And the rhythms broke loose again, the boy stood still, enraptured, then fished over a chair with his foot and straddled it, his arms crossed over the back, his head on his arms, his eyes ardently fastened on the box from which the miracle gushed forth.

Andreas felt like a second glass of beer, but it bothered him to have to disturb the barkeeper again. Why was he sitting here, anyway? In order to think things over? He could have done that a lot more easily in Munich and was accomplishing as little here as he would have there. But since he'd decided to do things this way, he wanted to see it through. The worst was yet to come.

Miep is dead, but Daniel is still alive. The murderers have passed him over. Is it possible that they're forgetting a Jew? Keeping him in prison until the end of the war? He knows it's not possible, yet he tries to convince himself for two whole days. Even a person who prides himself on uncompromising thought is capable of self-deception. He's ashamed of his chess playing, but can't leave it alone. Everything can still work out all right if black wins. Can you even say "everything," now, after Miep's death? Too much has happened already. And it always ends in a draw.

After a few days, the tom-toms drum the news that Daniel has been taken from the prison to the Schouwburg, to the theater that serves as a collection center for Jews. They don't forget Jews. A Jew is something to be deported.

Is deportation certain death? Is the East really nothingness? Can Germany afford to kill young men who are able to work?

He says this word "kill" to himself over and over again, softly, without moving his lips, he prays it at night in order to cast a spell over it, so that it can't come true. And again he takes out the chessboard. This afternoon, black wins; he's played the same game as always, but has suddenly realized that he can take the pawn with which white protects his king ahead of time, by a clever maneuver with bishop and knight.

He's wide awake, thinking more clearly than in the past, taking in the whole situation without deceiving himself about how dreadful it is, but is not prepared to give up hope as long as Daniel is in Holland.

A few times, Miep has told about people who managed to get away from the Schouwburg. Couldn't that still be possible? Without a firm plan, he tries to make contacts with people from the Jewish Council and the resistance movement, even finds himself talking to Germans. One person hands him on to the next, the subterranean threads are tightly spun and he discovers to his astonishment how many are able to find their way in this tangle that seems so impenetrable for him. They're playing a game whose rules they all seem to have mastered; he's the only one who has to leave his efforts to chance. What he learns doesn't sound bad: with money everything seems possible. Of course, fantastic sums are named, there's talk of twenty thousand, fifty thousand, even a hundred thousand guldens. A ridiculously small sum in comparison with what can be bought for it. But money is always ridiculous in relation to the life of a human being, provided you have it. He didn't.

Three days till the next transport leaves—too little time to travel to his mother, the only person who could give him the amount needed. So there's nothing left but to ask Daisy for it, naturally he only wants to borrow it, will pay it back as soon as he's gotten it from Mama. She's kind and understanding, doesn't resent his crudeness, but says it's impossible to ask her husband for more than five thousand.

The next morning she brings eight thousand—five from her husband and she's sold a piece of jewelry for three. In the meantime, however, he's learned from a member of the Jewish Council that there's a young SS man among the Schouwburg guards who can be bought for a thousand guldens. That much he has himself.

He puts the thousand in his pocket, along with the forged identity papers he's obtained for Daniel from the underground. Daisy's eight thousand he slips into his wallet, just in case.

He forbids himself to think that perhaps he'll soon see Daniel again, concentrates entirely on the bribery, what he'll say, how he'll lead up to it so he won't mess it up. Would it be better to put the money in an envelope? Between the pages of a newspaper? (To be on the safe side, he buys both.) Should he say "Heil Hitler" as a greeting or "good morning"? Is it a good idea to talk about the weather first, or Germany? (Home always summons up good sentiments. Or will feelings simply be disturbing in this business?) His acquaintance has told the SS man only that a German wants to talk to him, but not the reason.

When he enters the Schouwburg and finds his man waiting punctually in the box office—which smells of disinfectant—he doesn't need to waste many words. After just a few sentences, the handsome, uniformed fellow with the brazen child's face realizes what it's all about. Says he personally doesn't have a thing against the Jews, as far as he's concerned, they can stay put in Amsterdam. On the eastern front his leg was all shot up, and—he points to his cane—that's why he's here now, carrying out duties unworthy of a man. He only takes money because the risk to him is so great; and besides, he really does need it, because one's not likely to get a girl in this stupid country without paying.

All the talk is making Andreas even more nervous than he already is. Finally he puts a stop to it by pulling the thousand guldens out of his pocket and thrusting them into the other man's hand. The latter asks anxiously whether he can be relied on absolutely, even if things go wrong.

He gives his word of honor, which visibly calms the fellow, and then finally it comes down to the point where he can give Daniel's name.

The words are scarcely out of his mouth when disappointment shows on the insolent face. "Him? But he left last evening. He wasn't sent to a work brigade like the others, he was actually a criminal. They took him to the concentration camp, to Mauthausen."

Andreas doesn't start to scream, he stands there quietly, while the pain goes through his body in waves. And he doesn't fall over dead, as he would have expected to and certainly longed to, but is even able to understand the words being directed to him: "Now you want your money back, I suppose? Or can I offer you another Jew?"

He nods, but of course he'd like to free another Jew, preferably all of them. If he just didn't need to have anything more to do with the whole business! But things aren't made that easy for him—a list is pressed into his hand and he realizes that he's supposed to play fate. He holds the list close before his eyes, even though he's not near-sighted; it's a gesture of defense, as if his face were being threatened. At this distance he can see only indistinctly, the lines chase one another, slide right and left, toward top and bottom; only if he closes one eye can he read, and then only with considerable strain. Reads names. Pollack and Pollock and Praag. Turns to another page and finds a Carvalho between two Blumenfelds and several Cohens, has almost decided to take him, but suddenly begins to tremble—it's no good, he can't rescue a person just because he has a Spanish-sounding name. So he starts all over again, from the very beginning, sneaks a look over the list at the SS man to see if he's noticed the shaking, but maybe he didn't shake at all, maybe he just imagined it. Now he reads the column on the left side, where the dates of birth are listed. Three of the prisoners were born in 1925 like Daniel, one in the same month. "I'll take that one." For a moment he hopes it'll be a girl, he'd hate a girl less for having been set free in Daniel's place. With his index finger, he draws a line from the date to the name. Ruben, Joseph. Did he get the wrong line? Once again his finger travels horizontally across the page. The result is the same, can't make a girl out of it. He thinks about the first name and only when he discovers another whole row of Rubens, does he give the SS man the list and repeat: "That one there. Joseph Ruben."

He's told to wait outside at the stage door; it's made clear to him that everything has to be done very carefully. He leans against the wall beside the narrow door, the stucco flakes off. It's an old building, an old gray street from the turn of the century, ugly and without character.

A trolley car comes by, stops. People get out, the trolley starts up again and rolls away. A girl comes across the street toward him carrying a full shopping bag; he hasn't noticed whether she came on the trolley or on foot. She looks at him closely, hesitates a moment—at any rate, he has the impression she's hesitating. He's uncomfortable, turns his head away. When he looks around again, she's passed by.

It smells of disinfectant. The SS man limps across the box office, sticks the thousand guldens in his pocket, and says, "One moment please, the item you requested will be delivered immediately." Then he comes back with Daniel, whose hands are tied behind his back; he's been shaved bald as well. Andreas protests, he doesn't want someone who's tied up, that wasn't part of the bargain. "Tied up or not at all," says the SS man. "I can't risk my neck for your sake." Daniel looks straight ahead without smiling. Andreas doubts it's really Daniel. How can he find out for sure? He makes up his mind not to let himself be taken advantage of—he's not going to take the wrong person with him. Suddenly the door opens and a boy, who is trying hard to resist, is pushed out to him. At first, because of his small size, he takes him to be considerably younger; then he looks into the face of a sad, old monkey and is touched. He puts his arm around the small person, forces him to go along, and says, "We can't draw attention to ourselves."

When he speaks with his German accent, the resistance becomes stronger, the emaciated body tenses and resists, goes rigid. There is raging fear in the dark eyes.

"I'm not going to do anything to you, don't be so scared, I'm taking you home with me, you can stay there until it's all over, even if I am a German, you don't need to be afraid, I'm not a Nazi, absolutely not, just believe me, I like Jews a lot, there really are good Germans too." He's talking breathlessly and pulling him along despite his resistance. How is this poor child from the Jewish quarter to know that there are good Germans, too? He only knows murderers. "Do I look like a murderer. Look at me." But even the others don't look like murderers. What does a murderer look like, anyway? Like a human being. "Come on, just start to walk, put one foot in front of the other and stop howling. Here, take my handkerchief." Thank God, the Jewish face disappears behind the big kerchief. The two men in green uniforms on the opposite side of the street are looking over interestedly. Or maybe they see the star? No, the star is gone, the SS man with the limp appears to have thought about that. "Good, that's the way, I was beginning to think you couldn't walk anymore." Walk is an exaggeration; there are little, tapping steps beside him, from time to time a pulling at his hand. "Don't try to get away, where are you going to go? You won't be as safe anywhere as with me." Probably the other Rubenses are the boy's parents and brothers and sisters. He's robbed the poor monkey of the kindness that even the Gestapo murders show their victims, that of keeping families together in Holland. That's what comes of playing fate; he's picked the wrong one, one who likely doesn't even want freedom, who has no idea what to do with it. The very best thing he could do for him would be to take him right back to the Schouwburg. But that's no good, getting back in unnoticed might not be any easier than getting out, and he can't give the SS man away, he's given his word. "Why are you stopping? What are people going to think?" Kidnapping is what they'll think and they'll come running over to help the victim. "Come on, let's go."

He's completely done in, so much so that he no longer feels any pain. Only when he unlocks the door to the building do the tears run down his face. Now they're both crying, Joseph Ruben loudly and he quite softly.

In the apartment, all three women are standing in the vestibule. Sabine yells out: "That's the wrong one!" Daisy sobs, and only the van Lier woman does the right thing and pulls the little monkey to her huge breast without a word.

He gives Daisy her money back, then goes to his room. He doesn't need to close the door, no one dares follow him.

He takes a map of Europe from the bookshelf and looks for the place whose name he first heard from Sabine, along with the story—so unbelievable to him then—about the seven hundred death certificates for the seven hundred young men. He finds it, a little to the east of Linz, on the left bank of the Danube. Suddenly he remembers that he's heard of the place before; he's driven by it, though on the other side of the river, as a twelve-year-old, along with his parents. At a signpost, his father explained the meaning of the word "Maut," which amounted to the same thing as "toll," which was presumably to be paid there for the use of the ferry. At that time he was reading a lot about Greek mythology and connected the syllable and its uncanny "au" immediately with Charon, something that didn't fit in very well with the cheerful landscape, all those blossoming fruit trees, the baroque churches, and an already southerly blue sky.

It is there, then, that riding death stables his nag; he has to look for him there. He dare not think about what is to come now, as long as a remnant of the instinct for self-preservation is left in him. It is hell. His imagination takes up the enormous creative task—even if creative in a horribly perverted sense—and begins to picture what is going on in the huge slaughterhouse, and experiences it in ever-newer and increasingly horrible visions. And so he breaks himself on his own wheel, slowly and with refined cruelty. What is left is a human being who knows everything and can say nothing more, one who is mute in the face of reality.

The jazz blared on without an end, the hit tunes quavered on. His ears hurt, it was unbearable. But he just sat there without moving, without ordering a beer. And waited.

149

Chapter 17

H E was going to visit a grave again. This time without flowers, although he wouldn't have been deceiving the dead with them—no one was lying beneath the black marble block on which, in gold letters, was the name of the colonial official, together with the date of his birth and the fictitious date of his death. Branches of a weeping willow drooped above the stone and ivy climbed over it. In a pottery vase stood faded roses; beside it lay a wilted bouquet of tulips.

That was what he'd wanted to see. Daisy and Mejuffrouw van Lier were still coming here punctually on the anniversary of death indicated on the stone; so they were still living and had probably long since repressed the fact that he'd thrown the body of their father and employer into the canal with their consent. Everything was as it should be again: absolutely proper and bourgeoise. They'd forgotten the war, the whole terrible time—and even their own magnanimity.

When even the van Lier woman had to admit that Daniel wasn't going to come back ("Not before the end of the war," she said every time, and it sounded as if she wanted to conjure away fate with an incantation), she announced one day that she was not of a mind to stay in Amsterdam any longer: a sick brother in Bussum urgently needed her help and the country air might even do Jossele (that's what she called Joseph, her new child) some good.

"And what about me?" asked Sabine indignantly. "I guess I don't matter to you?"

"Herr Andreas can look after you from now on."

"Him? Just look at him. He can't even look after himself."

The van Lier woman could see that, of course, but wasn't about to be dissuaded from her plan, which included a new hiding place for Sabine that had been found by friends of Miep's, in the home of a young married couple in the country. The same friends had come up with a room for Andreas, on the Prinsengracht, near the Westerkerk. It was a small, bright room with built-in furniture painted gray and a view of a garden in which a magnolia was blooming when he moved in, and which, in addition, served as a place for his landlady to keep chickens. (She actually took him in for the sake of the chickens, firmly convinced that a German would be able to help find feed. When this presumption proved false, she became visibly more reserved.)

Before the apartment on Beethovenstraat could be vacated, the colonial official had to die, which took place with the help of the doctor who was already in on things and a funeral home whose owner belonged to a resistance group. Daisy came in black, this time accompanied by her husband, who wore a mourning band on his sleeve and reproached the van Lier woman for the fact that the coffin was already closed so that he couldn't see his father-in-law again. The Mejuffrouw, splendid in her black silk dress, glared over her nickel-rimmed glasses and silently served him wine and cake.

Andreas didn't want to go along, but Daisy insisted on it. "You owe that much to poor Papa." He gave in and rode behind the hearse in a rented car with its black curtains pulled down, together with the family and the van Lier woman.

In the coffin lay rocks packed in cotton wool. Since it was a long way to the grave, the four pallbearers had a hard time carrying it. Not many people had come (while walking he counted them—it came to seventeen in all, not including the pallbearers), there was no memorial service in the hall, no *Largo*, and no top hats. After they'd taken up a semicircular position around the grave, the minister of a reform congregation spoke. Andreas looked up at the gray sky and thought that if he didn't get a move on they were all going to get wet. But the pastor was in no hurry; with an unctuous and well-practiced voice he portrayed the life of the departed. Finally he spread his arms and said with a transfigured look, "Soul of man, how like unto water thou art." That would make an effective stopping point—Andreas hoped it was. But his hope was deceived: quite the contrary, the quotation from Goethe provided a new beginning, an inexhaustible theme, the preacher was quite taken by the subject of water, it surged through his words in the form of ocean, river, brook, and even as "our canals." Andreas glanced at Daisy. She was standing there, sobbing, the handkerchief pressed to her face. Suddenly she sneaked a look around the edge of the kerchief with one eye and winked at him. Only then did it become clear that she was laughing, and for a long moment, he loved her again the way he did at the beginning of their relationship.

He winked back, but remained serious. Patent leather shoes were floating away on the water like Ophelia's flowers, mossy, clammy, clinging weeds were growing out of bleached bones, young rats were playing with a medal. But then, as the first drops were falling and the coffin was being lowered into the grave, there was a muted, banging sound, and he had to fight against an irresistible urge to laugh, so much so that his eyes filled with tears from the strain. For the first time in months he was laughing—the grotesque had broken through the pain, there was something that kept him from thinking of Daniel, a realization that was more depressing than comforting.

On the next day he moved into his quarters on the Prinsengracht, where he remained until the end of the war. Went on writing his articles in order not to have to go to the front, and occasionally did courier duty for the resistance movement; they considered him— though he didn't join any of their organizations—reliable and called on him if there was something to be done which the bearer of a German passport could carry out less conspicuously than anyone else.

He was convinced that Daniel was dead, but every now and again he resisted the idea, considered it impossible. These rare outbreaks of hope were strengthened by the optimism of the Dutch, who almost all shared Sabine's opinion that the seven hundred death notices from Mauthausen were an act of sadism directed against the relatives. Only after Auschwitz had been taken by the Russians and the reports of gas chambers and crematoriums sent over Radio Oranje did they have to revise that view, but even then there were many who still didn't believe it and thought all the horrors and millions of dead were Communist propaganda.

A few months earlier, in September 1944, Andreas had been called up for military duty; allowances were no longer made for weak hearts, and even newspaper articles about Holland were no longer needed. He had his landlady take the notice to the local command post, where she claimed that two weeks before, he'd started out on a one-day trip to Germany from which he'd never returned. Since, at the time, the Allies had advanced quite far and had almost completely isolated the northern provinces of Holland, they believed her and just said that if he unexpectedly came back anyway, he should report immediately. And so he could go on living in his room without any great danger; nevertheless he very seldom went out, and, in the company of his landlady, ate sugar beets which were practically the only food that could still be obtained.

On New Year's Eve, the ships' whistles blew for an hour in the nearby harbor; the soldiers shot off their ammunition into the air for an hour. The war couldn't last many more months. Then we've won, thought the Dutch. Then we can go home, thought the Germans. Then the time of remaining mute will be over, thought Andreas, as he walked toward the harbor, attracted by the noise. Then he'd have to tell about what he'd been doing all these years. But it would be impossible to just stand right up and claim that he'd died, not just once, but over and over again each day, in the accursed camp, and that he'd used his time trying to imagine what the camp was, to let it take shape from the amorphous mass of fear that overcame everyone at the mere mention of the name, until it stood there in its death-bringing perfection and he, the sole victim, the sole executioner, could get on with the dying and killing. So he'd say nothing more than the fact that he'd spent those years by not writing anymore.

But he had to write again. Should all the effort of surviving turn out to have been in vain? It was important to find a way of rejoining the world.

He wasn't young enough anymore.

Young enough to have something to say. There were so few of his generation left that every single voice counted.

People have gone deaf from the shrill noise of the locusts and won't hear the voices. They should just let him be silent.

To be silent now would be cowardice and he's not a coward. He must give an account of what he'd seen. He should tell what he'd witnessed.

If he were asked, he'd speak.

No one would ask him.

Without being asked, he couldn't say anything.

Everyone had answers to questions. But he had to say exactly what no one thought to ask.

And what if he forgot something? How could the story be complete if everything wasn't told. What good would it do to talk about the rolling of the trolleys and forget a woman's scream. What would the rolling of the trolleys tell us without the scream? And if he mentioned the scream, a child's crying would be missing. And if he told about the child's crying, the flashlights would still be dark. In a made-up story you could leave a few things out. As a witness, you couldn't leave out a thing. Who can judge what's important and what's not? No, he couldn't be a witness.

But on the way home, he was already taking stock of this New Year's Eve, in order to use it as the beginning of the end in his testimony.

When the end had really come and the entry of the Canadian troops was expected at any moment, the landlady announced to him that he had to leave her house; he could now go back to Germany without difficulty, but she'd finally had enough of this illegal activity and wanted to have one of the liberators billetted in her house. Vainly, he tried to make her understand that he had to wait for news about Daniel. That was just one of his crazy ideas, he couldn't seriously believe the boy was still alive; and if he really did come back, Germany wasn't located on the other side of the world.

He was walking dejectedly through the city when he caught sight of a little hat with a veil in the dense crowd on Kalverstraat, ran after it, and grabbed Sabine by the sleeve. She threw her arms around his neck with a cry of joy and told, beaming, how she'd come back right after the capitulation and moved into her studio again. The Nazis living there had taken off in a cloud of dust, leaving her furniture behind. A person's just got to have some luck sometime. How 'bout him? Why was he wearing such a sad face? Maybe he felt like he was a German after all and wasn't so happy about who won the war? Daniel, oh, right, of course, he wanted to wait for Daniel and didn't know where? But it went without saying, he could hide out at her place, with the greatest pleasure, the tables were turned, life was just so crazy it was funny.

There he was, living on Beethovenstraat again—even if one floor higher—and patiently enduring Sabine's chatter; he was grateful to her, cooked for her out of gratitude, washed her dishes, swept the rooms, and, out of gratitude, didn't kick her when she strained his nerves to the breaking point. Almost every day she went out to look at the lists for him, those of the returnees and the much more extensive ones of the dead. But every time she came back without having found Daniel's name. Finally, she posted a notice in the refugee center, saying that Sabine Lisser was looking for Daniel Rosenbusch or any news about him.

Then, once, after she'd just left, the doorbell rang, and, although she'd forbidden it, he opened the door. There stood Daniel, ragged, emaciated, disheveled, in khaki pants and a windbreaker. But the illusion lasted too short a time to transform shock into joy; the round, very cool eyes of a stranger were looking at him. In the same instant, he realized that it was a girl standing in front of him.

"I'm Susanne Rosenbusch," she said in her rough, captivating voice. "Daniel Rosenbusch's cousin. Frau Lisser has posted a notice that she's looking for Daniel. Is Frau Lisser at home?"

Without answering, he took both her hands.

"What do you know about Daniel?"

"I? About Daniel? Not a thing. I've just returned today. From Auschwitz. There's no one else left of my family. When I read the notice, I thought that someone who's interested in Daniel might take me in for a while."

Overwhelmed by pity, he led her into the apartment. Not a thought for the people she had on her conscience. She was poor. She was beautiful. And she looked like Daniel. He took her in his arms and covered her face with kisses. She didn't protest, just laughed in amazement, then returned his tenderness.

"You certainly don't waste any time," she said eventually and pushed him away. "Who are you, anyway?"

From that hour on, they stayed together. At first with Sabine, then later in the room assigned to Susanne by some committee.

Now Susanne went to look at the lists. Soon she found the names of her and Daniel's parents among those of the dead. But not Daniel's. No one who returned knew anything about him. No news of Daniel. Nothing.

Chapter 18

H E packed his suitcase. In ten minutes he was finished. Right on top he put a notebook that was half filled. Black oil-cloth enclosed beginnings, trolley cars, four hundred human beings. Amsterdam hadn't helped him. Nothing had come to light that he hadn't already known. He just went on drifting between that which could not be told and the urge to tell it anyway.

He let the lock snap shut and pulled the belt tight. It had to be possible to get even closer to the past. To suspend time. To fill the void with pain again. To die once more and again and again and thereby find the words. Then he made up his mind to go to Mauthausen.

In order to avoid Munich, he drove to Linz via Bregenz and Innsbruck. Across the Danube and downstream on the left shore.

The fruit trees were in bloom, just as they were when he'd passed by with his parents. He couldn't recall having ever seen a more blissful landscape.

The road led away from the river, up hill and down, through meadows. He thought about how he was going to find the camp without asking for directions. Asking seemed out of the question to him. What should he say? Where's the camp, the former camp, was there a camp around here, the concentration camp, the place of murder, hell? What would a young farmer say if you asked him for directions to hell? Having to ask an older one would be even worse; to look into eyes that had been there and seen how they herded the prisoners away from the railroad station. Or from there to the stone quarries. It wouldn't work. Don't ask. Better to spend hours looking.

But as he rounded a curve, he saw it, high up, on a hill. Just walls, almost like a medieval fortress, but ugly. He was surprised that it was up so high; he'd always imagined it on a plain. Or even more, on a steppe. But naturally there was no such thing here.

At every crossroads now there was a signpost with the inscription: Camp Mauthausen. Painted in white on a barn: "Mauthausen—a warning"; on a wooden fence: "Never again." Questions became unnecessary. He was driving up to a memorial, in front of which, as he arrived up above, a bus was parking.

Previously he'd driven by a stone quarry that looked like all other stone quarries. You can't tell just by looking at a quarry whether murders have been committed there, you can only see that stones are being quarried. He didn't even know for sure whether this one had been used by the camp.

So, up there, where there was a splendid view, stood a bus with the "D" for Deutschland on the license plate and the city designation "A."

He climbed out, thought Susanne's red Porsche was out of place, but was honest enough to admit that a Volkswagen would have been no less so—nor, even, arriving on foot. It just wasn't right to tour a concentration camp. And "memorial park" was nothing other than a philistine translation of *sightseeing*, a much more precise word.

He went in through the gate, saw immediately that he was only in a sort of courtyard. Through two high walls, a bumpy path led up to an open space where memorial tablets and a large cross stood. The gateway to the actual camp was narrow. He entered a large square area with many stone barracks standing at right angles to the entrance, with grass growing between them. Everything looked very clean, neat, and completely unused. In the background, boys and girls were walking around, and the voice of an unseen teacher was explaining things.

He'd taken a few steps to the left (really only to have something to do), when a man walked up and spoke to him. His ears failed him, he could hear sounds, but not words. Patiently, they were repeated in French and when that had no effect, in English. Then finally he understood the sentence "*You have to pay, Sir, may I give you your ticket?*" He shook his head (He would have shaken his head at anything), then it dawned on him that he was supposed to pay. Two or three or four schillings—he was no longer paying attention to the amount—for something that he'd paid for with his whole life. He held out a bill to the man and waved away the change that was offered. Received a blue, carefully torn ticket. "*Please begin to the right,*" the man said in English. He turned to the right where a tablet had been placed in the wall and began to read: "Here the prisoners' hands…" Suddenly, he couldn't see anything more (though his eyes were dry). With a moan of distress, he turned and ran away.

Running back down, he thought: I can flee, Daniel couldn't, not Daniel.

Out of breath, he sat down on a rock in the parking lot.

He could think "view" and "Danube" and "silvery and beautiful." What had he expected? He didn't know. He knew even less than before.

After a little while, the boys and girls came out, along with their teacher, who was not much older than his pupils. They were talking a lot, all at the same time, about the camp, about not understanding their parents' generation, but also, as much as he could make out from snatches of conversation, about the excursion to the Raxalp planned for the next day.

Then they climbed in; he watched the bus drive away.

The slow realization that Daniel was dead and that he was alive. He hadn't died there as he'd always believed. He hadn't died at all.

He'd been wrong the whole time. He'd never been Daniel. Where was he? Where wasn't he? Can you start over again from the beginning?

He drove down into the village and onto the waiting ferry. Seen close-up, the rapidly flowing water wasn't silvery, but dirty gray. He stared into it and wished the boat ride would never end.

Then, when the ferry had nearly reached the opposite shore, he tore himself from the railing and gazed back at the camp that crowned the hill and looked like God knows what. But it was nothing. No one who saw it would get even the least idea about its past. No one would get an answer to the question of how it had been possible. The murdered had taken their secret and that of their murderers with them.

One shouldn't even talk about it. Nothing came of that. Words made nothing clear, they only covered things over.

But it was not good to leave it standing there. Ready to be used. It should have been torn down. Because it is bad to make things too easy for evil.

About the Author

GRETE WEIL was born in 1906. She married Edgar Weil in 1932, emigrating with him to Holland after the Nazis came to power. When her husband was arrested in 1941, Weil supported herself as a professional photographer, then went into hiding; it was during this period that she produced her first literary work, a marionette play for fellow fugitives entitled *The Christmas Legend 1943*. She returned to Germany in 1947 and now lives near Munich. Grete Weil is the author of five novels (including *The Bride Price,* which was published by David R. Godine in 1992), a collection of short stories, and two libretti, and has translated works by Lawrence Durrell, Conrad Aiken, and John Hawkes, among others. She has been the recipient of three literary awards, including the Scholl Prize.

About the Translator

JOHN BARRETT worked for many years as a cardiologist before turning to translation with Grete Weil's *The Bride Price,* which was named an Outstanding Translation of the Year by the American Literary Translators Association. He lives in New Hampshire.

Last Trolley from Beethovenstraat

was set in Bembo, a typeface based on the types used by Venetian scholar-publisher Aldus Manutius in the printing of *De Aetna,* written by Pietro Bembo and published in 1495. The original characters were cut in 1490 by Francesco Griffo, who at Aldus's request later cut the first italic types. Originally adapted by the English Monotype Company, Bembo is one of the most elegant, readable, and widely used of all book faces.

Book design by Roger Gordy.

Also available in Verba Mundi editions

THE BOOK OF NIGHTS by Sylvie Germain
translated from the French by Christine Donougher

Winner of six literary prizes, this novel combines the timeless power of medieval legend, the resonance of Greek tragedy, and the harsh immediacy of a newsreel. Germain traces a century in the life of the Peniel family, from the Franco-Prussian War to World War II — a tale of triumph and loss, eroticism and holocaust, and the endless cycle of birth and death. *"Original and compelling...Takes [magic and realism] to the outer limit and then fearlessly hurls one against the other."* — New York Times Book Review *(Notable Book of the Year, 1993)*

ISBN: 0-87923-975-1; 272 pages, hardcover; $22.95

THE CHRISTMAS ORATORIO by Göran Tunström
translated from the Swedish by Paul Hoover

A grand fresco of striving, ambition, grief, madness, and desire by Sweden's foremost contemporary novelist. Winner of the Nordic Council Prize, it unravels a three-generational saga as elaborate as a Bach cantata and engrossing as a Bergman film. *"This is a wonderful novel, crammed with vivid and surprising incidents...Like Bach's great musical work, Tunström's* Oratorio *offers a celebration of things that endure."* (Washington Times). *"Imaginary, dreamlike, rich in symbolism."* (Bloomsbury Review).

ISBN: 1-56792-008-X; 352 pages, hardcover; $23.95

THE PROSPECTOR by J. M. G. Le Clézio
translated from the French by Carol Marks

This "hypnotic and mythic" novel *(ALA Booklist)* is Le Clézio's masterpiece. It tells of one man's obsessive search—which leads him from a lush tropical island to the hell of World War I—for a legendary buried treasure, and through it for the "lost gold" of his childhood. *"A novel of intense beauty."* — Review of Contemporary Fiction

ISBN: 0-87923-976-X; 352 pages, hardcover; $22.95

THE LONELY YEARS, 1925-1939 by Isaac Babel
with a new introduction by Nathalie Babel
translated from the Russian by Andrew R. MacAndrew and Max Hayward

Long out of print, this is Babel's autobiography in letters, from his first sucess to his disappearance under Stalin. The introduction by Nathalie Babel, the writer's daughter, offers new information on Babel's personal relations, and uses previously unreleased information from KGB files to solve the mystery of his death. Includes 16 pages of photos. *"One of the literary masters of our century."* — Irving Howe

ISBN: 0-87923-978-6; 448 pages, softcover; $15.95

THE OBSCENE BIRD OF NIGHT by José Donoso
translated from the Spanish by Hardie St. Martin and Leonard Mades

Called "one of the great novels not only of Spanish America, but of our time" by Carlos Fuentes and "a masterpiece" by Luis Buñuel, this is the book that established Donoso as one of Latin America's greatest contemporary writers. *"The story line is like a great puzzle...invested with a vibrant, almost tangible reality."* — New York Times

ISBN: 1-56792-046-2; 448 pages, softcover; $15.95

HONEYMOON by Patrick Modiano
translated from the French by Barbara Wright

Modiano, winner of the Prix Goncourt, constructs "a haunting tale of quiet intensity" (*Review of Contmporary Fiction*). It parallels the story of Jean B., a filmmaker who abandons wife and career to hole up in a Paris hotel, with that of Ingrid and Rigaud, a refugee couple he'd met years before, and whose mystery continues to haunt him. *"His writing has the spare strength and telling concentration of a Simenon."* — The Independent

ISBN: 0-87923-947-6; 128 pages, hardcover; $19.95

THE TARTAR STEPPE by Dino Buzzati
translated from the Italian by Stuart C. Hood

A seminal work of 20th-century literature — at once an allegory of fascism, a critique of military life, and a chilling meditation on the human thirst for glory. *"Undoubtedly a masterpiece...[Buzzati] has brought to life a universal man and cast his being in surroundings which are familar to us all...It is a sublime book and Buzzati a master of the written word."* — Sunday Times

ISBN: 0-87923-992-1; 224 pages, softcover; $13.95

Verba Mundi books are available in the finer bookstores or directly from the publisher. To order, please call 1-800-344-4771, or send prepayment for the titles desired plus $4.50 postage and handling to:

David R. Godine, Publisher
Box 9103
Lincoln, Massachusetts 01773